# PāNCH(חָמֵשׁ)

Amit Saxena

**First published in 2021 by**

**Becomeshakespeare.com**

One Point Six Technologies Pvt Ltd.
119-123, 1st Floor, Building J2, B - Wing,
WadalaTruck Terminal, Wadala East, Mumbai,
Maharashtra, India, 400022.
T:+91 8080226699



ISBN - 978-93-5438-002-0

# Table of Content

# Hatchet Man

A tall, well-built man in his early thirties was standing by the door. His fair, glowing skin and light green eyes gave him the look of an ancient roman god.  A personality that is hard to forget.

The heavy rain during the night was soaking his long raincoat, boots, and hat. He was relaxed  yet a bit annoyed about something. He waited patiently for some time for the door to be opened , within the house, a middle-aged man with prosthetic hand and a leg made of wood came out. He resembled a pirate with an eye patch and was wearing a light shirt, jeans, and a cowboy boot. With the help of a wooden stick having an eagle face handle made of hard yellow translucent glass he welcomed the visitor   to enter his den.

The house was a big mansion with  two sets of identical stairs parallelly  going to the first floor and the second floor. They were made of wood and covered with furry carpets.

While the furniture looked antique and royal, it seemed to be never dry cleaned and so did the tiger head wall décor. Once a ferocious beast, it was now the house of a spider. Expensive items were all over the place, but everything appeared grim.

Soon enough, the sound of ice in the glass while drinking alcohol was hindering the silence. The place was quiet otherwise, and so were they! A few minutes later, suddenly the man stood up and slit the throat of the owner without a warning. Blood kept oozing out of the dead body like a fountain while the man seemed to enjoy his drink sitting on the chair. In a few minutes, the furry carpet was soaked with the blood of the owner and the visitor looked at the lifeless body with a smile. He left the house at ease with pride in his walk and called the cops that the owner had died.

While walking down the road he heard the police siren. An officer stopped him and inquired if he heard anything unusual to which the man unashamedly denied. He could see an ambulance rushing to the spot while he sat in the car knowing they will only find the bones covered with muscles wrapped in cloths. Lighting his cigarette, he took out his phone to talk to someone while he drove away from the scene in his car.

Soon he reached the seaport on the right to find a boat that will carry him to a safe location from where he will board his flight to his destination. The rain had stopped by now but his way to the boat was a bit difficult due to the wet mud that was sinking his boots inside.

Disembarking the plane at dawn he knew his task was over and he would finally meet his girlfriend Elizabeth after a week. Meeting Elizabeth each time was just like meeting her after decades, due to all the shower of kisses, hugs, and romantic words she couldn't stop at that time. In her early thirties, she had the perfect body a man always dreams of! She was fair, tall and had blue eyes. The world was forgotten, and the only world was in her eyes where he wanted to be for the rest of his life. Her lips were as soft as a feather and her breath was heavy and hot. While she played with his hair, he was playing with her body tasting every inch like it was as sweet as honey and as delicate as a flower. They were so much into each other that they didn't notice the arrival of dawn .

"Oliver, breakfast is ready, darling," Elizabeth was excited to have this meal together after a long time. Coming out of the steamy bath covering his lower body with a towel, he kissed her forehead and sat near her for breakfast. Elizabeth was excited to know about his tour and the sales meet with his clients so she was filled with questions. While Oliver, who was afraid to reveal the real reason of his visit, was trying to evade her intrusions. But it seemed that she was eager to hear his stories. Deep down Elizabeth had a suspicion that Oliver was cheating on her and Oliver was thinking about how he could avoid telling her his real profession. He was not a Sales Representative working with a Diamond company, he was a hitman, a cold-blooded hitman who was a wanted criminal in many countries but because of his sheer wit and cynicism, was untraceable.

In a hurry, he completed his breakfast, changed his clothes, and rushed out of the house pretending to be late for his meeting. Sitting in his car, he took a deep breath and tried to think about Elizabeth's reaction if she came to know about his real profession.

Reaching his destination, he met a person with curly hair, a huge paunch, tan skin with a deep cut on his left cheek. The man handed over an envelope to him. It had a picture of his next target and flipping the picture, Oliver found all the information he required. Then, he gave another envelope which contained the advance fees. Finding that the fees in the envelope was lower than the agreed amount, Oliver got very angry and he refused the task. Half an hour after bargaining, Oliver accepted the offer and left. The person escorted him to the car and after leaving

Oliver called from his mobile and informed him that the task will be completed soon.

Waiting at the Café for the clock to hit 6 P.M., Oliver started planning the execution of his new task. Suddenly Elizabeth came into his thoughts. He knew she will be upset and might create a scene forcing him to avoid this trip. He looked at her picture on his phone and said, "This is the only thing I know and am good at".

Reaching home, he found Elizabeth having a bath. Taking advantage of this, he quickly removed his clothes and jumped into the shower with her, where they both played with each other. At the dinner table, he took the shot by stating that he needed money to pay the rent of the condo, and other bills, but with his salary he couldn't. He explained to her that he must go on sales calls, as each will give him a good commission, which will help him in meeting his ends. Elizabeth who was blind in his love was a fan of his commitment towards his work, and she happily agreed to support his next tour's cause. Unaware, that the smile on her face will soon snatch away the smiles of many.

Reaching the town where he was going to kill his target, Oliver waited for the right time. His targets name was Justin, and he was a contractor. The person who wanted to eliminate him was his younger brother and his partner. Oliver never asked the reason why his clients wanted to kill their targets. The only thing he cared was the amount. He did not take credits, and demanded the whole amount before the work was done. If the work was not done because of any problem, (which usually never happened), Oliver used to promise that he would pay double the amount paid to him. After a week of following Justin, he was now ready to strike. In the evening his target was in a pub drinking heavily where Oliver introduced himself as Alexander, a rich investor and looking for a partner to open a business in the city, and asked if he could join him.

On this, his target showed interest, and they discussed further on it. In some time, they became friends and Justin urged Oliver, aka Alexander, to come over to his place to discuss the proposal further with drinks. He even requested Alexander to stay overnight, but he refused. So, they sat together at the pub and discussed the venture, but the focus was more on alcohol. Alexander was trying to get Justin drunker, so that he could execute his job perfectly.

Justin was unable to walk properly so Oliver held him and took him to his apartment. The apartment had 2 rooms with a small balcony. Oliver knew that his target lived with his wife and a 6-month-old kid, and that his wife is out for some work. On the shelf, he could see the standing photograph of his beautiful wife and their kid. Without further ado, he cleverly slit up his target's throat and with a smile left the apartment. While leaving he called up the cops and informed them about the lifeless body.

With no hurry, he boarded the elevator, and went to the basement where his car was parked. Seated he removed the wig, mustache, and the fake mole on his right cheek, packed it in a bag, and threw it all on the back seat. While driving away, he could see the police car and the ambulance rushing to the crime scene. He then boarded his flight back to his home where he had safely left the love of his life.

Reaching at midnight, he found Elizabeth waiting for him. Her eyes were filled with excitement and eagerness to share something. While hugging him she placed a thing in his hand. It was a pregnancy kit that showed 2 red lines confirming that Elizabeth was pregnant. Oliver was going to become a father. The surprise was so huge that Oliver took some time to digest that news. He was confused as to whether he should cry or smile, thank her or congratulate her, hug her tight, or just stare at her! Elizabeth was laughing at his situation as she could see her hunk boyfriend behaving like a small child who has just been surprised with his much-awaited gift. She was thrilled and whispered in his ear, "You are going to be the father of my child". To which Oliver jumped, and sat down on the couch, asking for some time to digest and believe this news to be true, or just a prank on him. Collecting himself, Oliver confessed he didn't know how to read a pregnancy kit, and when she told him how to read, he took out his phone and searched it online again. He lost all his vocabulary and just stared at her with tears rolling down his cheeks. After dinner, the whole night she slept on his arm, while he was cuddling her just like a baby cuddles its soft toy.

Next morning, Elizabeth called out, "Oliver", to confirm his presence in the room. Once he replied, she went on stating that she needed to visit a gynecologist to discuss her pregnancy. Oliver agreed and asked her to drive slowly, to which she demanded him to ride her to the hospital and back. Even though Oliver had a meeting with his new client, he couldn't refuse her. So, he called his client and asked to delay the meeting by 3 hours. To his surprise, the client refused. As per him, Oliver had agreed for this work which had already delayed by months and any further delay meant losing this work. Oliver knew he had to choose either of the two. Once agreeing on a work, he never backed out, but he couldn't leave Elizabeth at this time when she needed him the most. So, the meeting was scheduled at the hospital. But Oliver could not afford to introduce his girlfriend to his client at any cost, So He asked his client to visit the hospital, introduce himself as his client, and introduce his target as a sub-client whom he should meet. Oliver cannot afford to introduce his wife to his client at any cost.

At the hospital, he asked his girlfriend to wait while he went to meet the new client. The client had an Indian accent and wore a turban, and he wanted to kill his own father so he could get the property in his name. They fixed the deal, and Oliver was ready for the work with lower fees than he usually charged.

Once done with the meeting he went back to his girlfriend. Upon reading the name of the doctor, Oliver began to think something. On being asked, he told Elizabeth that her name reminded him of a school friend who was very close to him.. After graduation, she had left for further education. Elizabeth was waiting for her turn when Oliver froze after seeing the doctor. She was the same Luke he was thinking about outside her cabin. Dr. Luke was a short lady with fair skin and golden hair. Meeting Oliver after a very long time, she jumped in excitement and hugged him tightly and began to recollect their old memories of school days. Meanwhile, Elizabeth felt a bit jealous and anxious about her checkup, and was getting restless. With every proceeding minute, her anger was  rising, and finally, she jumped into the middle of their conversation and asked Dr. Luke to do what she had come for. Neither

her voice nor her words were appreciated by either of the long-lost friends, but knowing Elizabeth for her temper Oliver decided to quietly sit and look apologetic towards Luke.

After the checkup, on the way back home, Elizabeth was very angry and throughout the drive was just shouting and yelling at Oliver. Whenever he tried to relax her, her temper would blast again. Oliver knew that it was just because she was going to become a mother so he tried to look after her that day and, in fact, was able to. He had to tell her that he needed to travel the following morning and thought that she would react and fight with him the whole night. But, to his surprise, she understood his situation and asked him to return early, if possible.

Oliver, on his way the next morning, was thinking about how he was going to perform his task, and with that, he was thinking about him becoming a father. He could hear the voice of a kid shouting "Papa", which made him emotional. He shook his head and tried to concentrate on his task.

After noticing the pattern of his target for a week, he chose a date and time to execute the killing. The same way he used to do for all his targets. This time was a bit special. He was going to be a father. The killing was not a task but art for him and he was an artist. A heartless artist, who would never think twice before snatching someone's life, today was filled with love and affection for the newborn who was coming in his life.

Getting back to the task at hand, Oliver killed his target the same way. Slit his throat and while leaving informed the cops about the murder. Reached his car and removed his wig, mustaches, and a mole on his right cheek. Now, his head, was filled only with the thoughts of his beautiful girlfriend and his child which she was carrying.

On the flight, Oliver was calculating his funds, mentally preparing a menu and guest list of who all will be invited on the day his child was to arrive in this world. He was very excited. He listed out many baby names but knew that Elizabeth will finally choose the name. At that time he ignored this and was simply happy choosing baby name and even starting to memorize it. He was the happiest person on that plane. Now, he wanted to marry Elizabeth and start his married life. He knew Elizabeth would want to marry him but then his real identity intervened, shattering his dreams. He knew that if Elizabeth found out that he is a hitman, she will never marry him, she may never even let him meet his child. His breath froze and he was breathing heavily. The passengers nearby alerted the crew and the crew tried to assist him. In a few minutes, he felt better and in some time the plane touched down. On his way home, he was thinking hard about how to avoid this situation but rejected the feeling of quitting, as this was the only profession he knew best.

He loved her and so did she. The feeling of loss was over taking his emotions which made him a bit agitated and made him fight on petty issues. It was clear he was not happy about something. The worst part was that he could not discuss it with anyone. He had to resolve it himself. Elizabeth while watching a sudden change in his behavior was a bit concerned and afraid. She knew Oliver could hit her if he loses his cool. Asking him may irritate him and keeping mum was killing her. Something was seriously wrong she knew it but was unable to find the cause.

She thought of calling his office to check what was wrong. She never had the numbers, nor the address. The name was incomplete so was not appearing on the websites. Elizabeth wanted to help him.  She loved him a lot and seeing him suffering was killing her. She went to him and confront him on his mood swings to which Oliver bluntly rejected and asked her not to worry. Upon asking his office details, Oliver asked why she needed those and then said she shouldn't take so much stress. A heated argument started between them on why he can't share the contact details of his office with her. Knowing this would come, Oliver became aggressive and threatened Elizabeth. The argument went on the whole night, but he did not share his office details.

The next morning, a sad and tired Elizabeth left the house and wrote a note that she will only come back once he tells her what was wrong with him, sharing the details of where he is working. When Oliver read the note in the afternoon, he knew what he thought in the flight was turning into reality. Afraid of the situation he decided to take his time, relax, and then respond. While doing his workout he could only hear his cry pleading Elizabeth not to leave him and not to snatch away his child from him.

Knowing the gravity of the situation he was very upset. Drinking since morning till late night, smoking cigarettes like a burning chimney in his lungs. He was not able to appreciate anything in life. Elizabeth leaving him was just like Oliver with a body but without a soul. It felt like a curse was following him.

At night while sleeping he could see the faces of the dead who were killed by him without mercy. He made their loved ones live a life which they didn't deserve. The dead would laugh at him in his sleep and say that what is happening to him is still not enough against what he had done. He should suffer more, feel the same pain that their families are still feeling every minute, every day. Their kids are living a life without their fathers.

They never deserved such a life. He could feel them cursing him, could hear their voices in his ears. The pangs of separation and the voices of the dead whom he killed ruthlessly were haunting him day and night. The disability of thinking due to this was forcing him to live like a zombie. There was not a single day when he was not thinking about her. Dreaming about Elizabeth, one day, he accidentally dropped a dumbbell on his leg and his bone broke. Lying on the floor in sheer pain, he managed to call for an ambulance.

At the hospital, after having sedatives to reduce the pain, he was getting a bit unconscious. In that situation, Oliver was pleading with Elizabeth to forgive him for what he had done with all his targets. He cried that he could see all of them are in his dreams and justifying his situation but also want more pain as it is not as much as they and their families faced. Hearing this, the hospital crew got suspicious and started to check his details. The staff found that his fingerprints matched a fugitive who was at large and most wanted. The biggest hitman was in front of them without a weapon but in vain.

At once the staff called the Police and informed them about him. Within 15 minutes, 5 police cars and 2 heavily armed units arrived to arrest Oliver. Officer Roger was the officer in-charge for this case. He was six feet, huge and dark complexioned man and his hair were all white. Bossy look, arrogant face and with a very unfriendly behavior he looked at Oliver. While taking out a of box cigarette, he flipped out one, tapped on his palm and place the bud on his mouth but looking at the No-Smoking sign and the frown on the nurse's face he put it back into the box, returned the box to his pocket and said "Your name is in the most wanted list and I am honored to catch you. You didn't give anyone the chance to catch your neck but here I am. You are nothing but a piece of unwanted shit. I will make sure to make your life very miserable and every minute you will regret being caught by me". He ordered his men to handcuff him with the bed, so he wouldn't run away.

"Now you will see how I will treat you. You are safe till you are here. I will break every bone of yours. Don't worry you will come back here soon" He said laughing at him, and again he took out his cigarette box but put it back when he saw the nurse's face frown again. Reaching the hospital, Elizabeth was bewildered as she was unable to understand what was going on. On learning that she knows the fugitive, they arrest her too. While being walked on the corridor of the hospital handcuffed, Elizabeth could see all eyes on her. She could hear people accusing her even if they didn't know who she was and why she was being taken. The feeling of being pushed and ordered by someone against our own will is very disappointing. Only one question was rising on her mind "Why is it happening to  me?"

Arriving at the police station, the officer asked her to deposit her belongings and to wait in a room. The room was small, it had a long table with three chairs. Two chairs were facing the table and the single chair was facing the other two chairs. There was a big hanging lamp which was just above the table. Elizabeth was asked to sit on the chair facing the two chairs and behind those chairs was a big mirror which was one-way window glass. By this glass the policemen can listen to the conversation and see what's going on, without anyone knowing they are watching. Waiting in the room, she asked for some water, but her request went unnoticed. After an hour a lady officer and a male officer entered the room. The lady officer was an African race, heavy built and was wearing a police uniform. The male officer was a fair skinned, obese man with short height, brown hair and was wearing a shirt and pant. They introduced themselves and advised Elizabeth that she was supposed to speak only the truth. Whatever she said would be cross verified and if she provided wrong information she will be arrested on grounds of punishable offense. Elizabeth was still unable to understand why she was detained and what was going on with her. She again requested for water and this time the lady officer gave her a water bottle. She opened the bottle and drank the water in a hurry. She was afraid and sweating. The lady officer started her interrogation:

Lady officer: Do you know why you are here?

Elizabeth: Sorry, but not a clue. I have been asking but no one is telling me anything.

Lady officer: Okay, why did you come to the hospital? Is there anyone you know?

Elizabeth: Yes, is it an offense? Is going to hospitals not legal now?

Male officer: "Criminals commit crimes and then they behave like innocents. Of course, it is an offense." His voice was rising," Killing people is illegal at least for us as we live in a society, but it seems for people like you who don't belong to this society, it's not illegal. Your place is not outside madam, it's here in the jail." He points towards the door.

The lady officer asked her colleague to calm down and continued her questioning

Lady officer: "Since when are you in this business? How many people have you killed?"

Elizabeth was shocked by this question. With a trembling voice she said, "Madam, I don't know what the hell you are saying? I have never killed a mouse and you are blaming me for murdering people?!" The lady officer looked at her with a smile and said, "First you criminals deny and then ya'll confess. Let see when you will break!" The male officer added "She is the best in this business. No other country has ever had a picture of her. She won't break and confess easily. We will have to use force on her". Agreeing to this the lady officer continued "The sooner you confess, the better it would be for you. I am sure you won't like the ways we may have to take to make you talk, (with a smile on her face) of course unless you are used to it."

Lady officer: "How do you know Alexander?"

Elizabeth : "Never heard this name. Who is this "Alexander"?"

At the hospital, the nurse comes to check on Oliver. Within a few seconds, she runs out to call the doctor. The constables who were guarding outside, became attentive, and rushed inside to check Oliver's ward. There they saw his dead body with his throat slit. The same way he used to kill others. The doctor, upon checking the body, confirmed that he was dead. Oliver had been killed. How and who did it, no one knew.

Lady officer: "The person whom you came to meet at the hospital Elizabeth. Now don't tell me you didn't know his name and you just came to visit him randomly."

Elizabeth: "I swear to god, I don't know this name. (With a pause) You mean Oliver? I came to meet Oliver ."

The mobile phone of the lady officer rang and when she answered it she found out that Oliver had been killed. His throat was slit. The killer was still at large, and they were investigating. The lady officer confirmed what she heard, disconnected the call, and kept the phone aside. She looked at the male officer and shared this news in his ear.

Quietly staring at Elizabeth, the lady officer noddded her head, asking her to continue. Elizabeth said, "Oliver is my boyfriend and he is a sales representative in a Diamond company. He is going to be the father of my child, but we are not married yet."

Lady officer: "So you guys have a part-time job also?" On this, the male officer laughed and added, "A nice way to cover up your crime".

The Lady officer continued "Elizabeth, I want to stress that you are in big shit. I am sure you will not want your child to be born in jail. You may want him to be born free and live as other children do. I am requesting you, for the sake of your child, tell us the truth. How did you meet Alexander and why did you join him?"

Elizabeth: "I came to meet Oliver and not Alexander. Here I guess you are mistaken with identity. You are looking for Alexander and unfortunately, Oliver comes under your radar due to which you are trying to implicate the blame on him and me. You are seriously making a mistake, madam."

Touching her forehead, the lady officer showed her Oliver's photographs. "We were following Alexander for a quite long time. Don't fool us. We know that he is Alexander and not Oliver. You need to co-operate or else I will leave. Another lady officer will come and then you will start talking like a parrot. You know why? She doesn't speak with her mouth. Her hands speak and you will better understand that language I am sure".

Frightened Elizabeth stared at the lady officer with tears rolling down her cheeks. Unable to understand what was going on, she again tried to stress that she didn't know Alexander. She called him Oliver which is the name she knew.

At the hospital, the doctors arranged for an autopsy. The officer in charge, Roger, arrived at the hospital and asked his men how it happened. "Either one of you or all of you have killed him. I swear to god, I won't leave a single stone unturned. I will expose the killer". The officer shouted and started lighting his cigarette but soon crushed it looking at the 'No-Smoking' sign. He asked the hospital security team to share the CCTV footage which was installed outside Alexander's ward.

Back at the police station, on being questioned how she met him, Elizabeth narrated her story. "I was doing my Business Administration Classes when I first met him. He was a shy guy, never spoke to anyone in a high tone, and was one of the most handsome guys in the class. I had feelings for him but was scared to face rejection. Last semester he finally approached me and proposed to me. I was waiting all these years and without wasting a minute I said yes. Since then it has been 12 years we have been together".

"12 years in a relationship and you didn't marry? Why?" the male officer asked.

"He wanted time. He wanted to build a base before going into marriage" Elizabeth answered.

Lady officer: "Don't you think it is illogical? I mean living for 12 years together and not marrying is itself a question mark on his intentions. You never felt so?"

Elizabeth shook her head from side to side  indicating a 'no'.

"Did you ever enquire about him? Asked his past, where he lived and where are his parents?" the male officer asked.

"He didn't have a past. I mean, he never had a girlfriend, I was his first. He lived here in this city alone. His parents died long ago in a car accident".

Lady officer: "Oh boy! You are a fool. He fooled you all these years. His name is Alexander to which he told you, Oliver, he has a long history of crime. He killed his parents and his elder sister at the age of 8, called the police to inform about this crime. It took us 2 years to catch him for these murders. He is very clever. He was sent to jail for 3 years and at the age of 13, he killed his girlfriend by slitting her throat. This crime was never proven on him. Lucky bastard. You know nothing. He might kill you too".

The officer checked the footage and circled one suspicious person entering the ward. In a few minutes, that person exited the ward, but walked in a very calm manner as if nothing had happened. The officer asked his men to find that person. "I want this person within 24 hours or all of you will be suspended and a criminal charge will be pressed on you all for criminal activity or helping in a criminal activity". His men saluted him and ran out in fear. The officer asked the doctor when could he get the autopsy report. The doctor said he needed 3 or 4 hours.

After 3 hours the doctors brought the report which confirmed that Alexander died due to excessive bleeding and the cause of death was by slit on his throat. There was no other mark on his body and yes, his leg bone was broken due to the fall of heavyweight.

They also confirmed that he couldn't be a father as his testicles were injured due to an extremely old injury. The body was ready to be collected for performing the last rites.

At the police station, Elizabeth was staring ahead, mum, with tears rolling down her cheeks. She started slapping herself for being such a fool in loving and believing someone so much. Started crying and shouting, "Oliver why did you do this to me?"

The two officers were sitting and looking at her with no expression. They were trained and had seen such fake tears a lot in all their careers.

Lady officer: "Elizabeth, please calm down. We are not interested in your stories, we just want to know how much you are involved in the crimes, your Modus operandi, and who else are involved. Help us and I assure you that I will try to reduce your sentence."

Within a few hours, the Police men received a clue about the murderer. They inform their boss and started searching for more clues. They received a tip from their informers about the hideout of that hitman and the race to catch him started soon enough. Arriving at the spot he was brought into custody. After hours of questioning, and breaking some of his bones, the hitman agreed to talk.

He told the officer that Alexander and he were friends since childhood. They first met at juvenile jail when he was serving a term for killing his family. He was never sorry for his doings and said that he would like to pursue this as a profession. He killed his family because they used to force him to do things he never wanted to do. He hated going to school and doing what all the other kids were doing. He always wanted to do something which would make him different from others and people would feel afraid of him.

He continued "I was so impressed with him that I decided that I will work only with him. He happily accepted my invitation and then we waited to get released from the jail. Both of us were going to get released in the same year and the same month but on different dates. After few years Alexander got a girlfriend. She was very sexy, but the only problem was that she never let him touch her. Tired of being just a boyfriend he needed to have sex with her. One evening he met me and expressed his dissatisfaction. I never wanted him to have a girlfriend, so I insisted that he need to sleep with her. I offered my help to convince her, to which he agreed.

The next day we reached her house. Alexander had the keys, so we entered the house. I asked Alexander to go to the shop and buy a pack of condoms. He left the house. When I climbed up the stairs for the upper room, I could hear the voice of the shower. The bathroom was open, and I could see her under the shower. She looked like a goddess. I lost my senses and jumped on her. She tried to resist but it was too late I had overpowered her. The bathroom was small, so she was trapped and I was able to satisfy my libido. I knew Alexander was about to come back so I killed her. I threw her in the bathtub in the next room and called Alexander to come fast. I told him that I found her drowned in the tub and he believed me. Later it was discovered that she was raped and murdered. Alexander was the prime suspect but had to be released as nothing was against him. Later we found another person who was just like us.

Three of us joined to form a group. One used to bring a lead, I was to follow the target and monitor their daily routine and Alexander was the person who decided the date, venue, and execution of the target. We only worked for those who could pay us the amount we demanded. Together we worked for more than 100 clients. Out of which only 3 failed to pay us the demanded amount. They all got killed. We believe in teamwork and never faced problems within. Never felt betrayed".

"Then why did you kill Alexander?" The officer asked. "He was in love. Love is the weakest thing on earth, and the most dangerous. He had to get killed or he would have gotten us killed".

Meanwhile, staring at the officers, Elizabeth challenged

"I have never committed any crime, I am not afraid of your threats. You don't have anything against me, so prove it and then you can kill me. I am not party to any such crime. Yes, I loved him, and his child is inside me but now knowing this I will not bring him to this world. His father killed him even before he is born".

The two officers left the room leaving Elizabeth with her tears rolling down her cheeks. A few moments later, she was asked to leave for her house. While exiting the premises, the lady officer called her and said "See, I am also a lady, I also fell in love once and my heart was also broken. Today, I am married with 2 kids at home and my husband loves me like anything and so do I. All I mean to say is, never curse yourself. Whatever you did was the best you could and sometimes, things are not as good as they seem to be. You loved him so much that you decided to have a child with him. There is nothing wrong with what you did, and please never blame your child for anything. He deserves to come to this world, to be loved, and looked after. Believe me, you will never forgive yourself if you do something to him. You may heal with the betrayal of love, but you may not be able to heal this loss."

At the Hospital,the officer partner about their third partner. Alexander's partner told him that Elizabeth was the third partner. There are now two Elizabeth , one whom he loved, and the other his partner. "Alexander told us that he was going to be a father. I knew that this was not his child". The officer asked him whose child was this. To which he replied "It was Elizabeth's". The police officer was surprised. "Elizabeth was a man, but with a body of a woman. Having a woman in the gang always made us look less suspicious, and when the woman has the power of a man, it's like the best of all! This was our secret as a female always can be used as a weapon to escape. I and Elizabeth, the partner, decided to kill his lover Elizabeth as we knew that Alexander was thinking of breaking up with us which was a threat to us. We killed her the day he had left to complete his recent task. We even left a note in his home saying that Elizabeth is leaving him because of his behavior. Elizabeth came to the hospital to kill him, but your officers arrested her, so I had to complete this task".

Knowing the interrogation with Elizabeth would end in sometime, the officer immediately took out his mobile and dialed the number of the lady officer.

With an empty face, Elizabeth left the premises and the officer watched  as she disappeared into the darkness of the night.

While trying to locate her in the darkness, her mobile

phone rang. Picking up the call she heard the officer asking "Don't let Elizabeth get away. He is the mastermind and by the way, he is a male and not a female". While listening to this the lady officer could not get a glimpse of the real culprit. She knew Elizabeth was gone. She will never be able to catch her again. Still, she tried to find her everywhere but was unable to. She looked at the mirror of her car and said, "Elizabeth you are not only intelligent but also exceedingly clever. I have seen many criminals but none of your level".

# Love Story

"I don't know why I married you!", Rohini shouted at Shaan." You are the biggest mistake I have ever made in my life. I wish I could turn the time wheel back and mend it" She continued while sobbing on her bed. Shaan was sedentary on a rocking chair, savoring a glass of his favorite whiskey. Rohini was sitting on the bed, watching Shaan helplessly. "Did you have your medicine? You have a habit of skipping it. Have it now, if you have not yet taken it", said Shaan while standing up and leaving the room to refill his glass with whisky.

Rohini, was a 29-year-old caring human being full of life. 5 feet 7 inches in height, she had a slim figure with fair skin and black hair. She was a scholar and had received a gold medal in economics. Her father was a government employee and got retired last year. He was not an old man but behaved like one. Always wearing a shawl over his shoulders, he had white hair and preferred wearing Kurta Pajama.

Her mother was a dean in a medical college and retired three months ago. Energetic in nature, she was always looked young and smart. She used to spend a good amount of time and money in parlors for the upkeep of her overall looks. Rohini also had a brother who was still pursuing civil entrance examinations. He tried thrice but was not selected and now he was trying for the fourth time and hoped to get through. Rohini loved Indian traditional clothes over western outfits. She used to wear western clothes, but she preferred more of the Indian ones.

Shaan was 31 years old, with a witty sense of humor, and respect for others, which made him an ideal friend one can ever dream of. 5 feet 11 inches in height with a muscular and sturdy built, he had tried competing for medical entrance exams but couldn't clear it. Finally, he completed his MBA in sales and marketing and now was searching for a job in the same.

His family was very poor since his father was a car garage mechanic by profession, while his mother was a housewife. Sometimes, Shaan's parents had to sleep empty stomach but never let their son's stomach to growl. They always tried to keep up with his demands even if they had to eat only once a day. His father was a hard worker but never had the zeal to excel in his life. He was happy with what he had, but wanted Shaan to live a better life than what he himself was living till now. Shaan had two elder brothers, but both had passed away a few years back in an accident. His father was still actively waged in the same garage where he started his career, and wanted to work till his body allowed.

The story of Rohini and Shaan meeting with each other was one of a kind. Six years ago, Rohini had gone with her friends to watch a movie. The movie was so boring that she had to leave the screen to recuperate, and thought of having some popcorn with a glass of cola. At the counter, Shaan was taking orders. Looking at Rohini for the first time, his heart started pounding louder than it used to. While delivering the order to Rohini, Shaan purposely handed her his mobile number with confidence without worrying about any of the consequences. Rohini took that paper, read, and then tore it into pieces and threw it in the dustbin while leaving the counter. Shaan was standing with a smile on his face. He knew that she has read his mobile number and must have memorized it.

The next day Shaan called Rohini on her mobile phone. Upon being enquired how he managed to get her number, he replied that he was able to get it through one of their common friends. He was desperate to tell her how he felt after meeting her for the first time. He went on and told her how he could hear his heartbeat pounding into his ear and how he was able to see the angel of love shooting him with the arrow of love with her name on it. He also asked for permission from her if he could call her again to which she agreed. His attitude and courage impressed her, and she also agreed to go out with him for a coffee. His sense of humor and respect for women compelled her to fall for him. Soon, their relationship kicked off and they started meeting more often.

One evening Rohini tried calling Shaan but his phone was switched off. Even after several attempts, his phone was still unreachable. After calling all his friends, one of them was able to give her a clue about where he might be. As per him, he may have gone to meet his parents who lived in a town that was in another state. The connectivity for that place is only via bus or train and the journey was about 12 hours with limited or very poor network signals. The friend explained that there might have been an emergency about which he couldn't have informed her.

Two days later, Rohini tried Shaan's number again, and this time it rang., He picked up her call. After checking with him about him and his family's wellbeing, Shaan told her that he was incarcerated. He was arrested by the police for drinking while driving and that being a weekend, he couldn't get bail. "My phone was confiscated by the police therefore, I couldn't inform you. Everything is good now and I am free", Shaan told her. She got annoyed and disconnected the phone on his face. Shaan tried her number but she didn't respond to any of his calls.

Rohini was very upset, but the fire of love was much higher than all the agony he gave her. She was in love with him and the love was unconditional, and she knew that Shaan also loved her a lot. He never took advantage even when she used to compel him to do the extremes, he was the one who repudiated. Usually, boys are the ones who initiate, and the girls are the ones to refuse, but in their case, it was the opposite. He loved her and always asked her to wait for the right time.

He desperately wanted to marry her. In fact, they both wanted to marry each other desperately, but both were searching for jobs, and had decided that they will marry each other after they get a job. Rohini's parents never objected to her having an affair with him and agreed to their decision about waiting till both got their jobs. Shaan's mother always quoted, "Love is a beautiful feeling but when you feel hungry and there is nothing to eat, love goes out of the window, and then there is only curse. Love is important but money is more important.

It's like a train where the engine is money and love is the bogie". Rohini knew whatever Shaan's mother said was correct and she had been through it.

Somewhere Rohini was thinking whether she was taking the right decision of marrying him. She thought of speaking with Shaan's mother. "Aunty, do you think we are doing the right thing? I mean marrying each other?" Shaan's mother looked at her and said "Beta, this is something you have to decide. You both are well educated and exceedingly smart. But I know that you will get a better job, better pay, and better opportunities in life, while my son, on the other hand, may not be as lucky as you are, and this may make things a little bitter. A male may not be able to see his wife doing better than him. Society looks upon these men as Inferior, and this might hurt their egos. If both of you can handle this, then there is nothing that can stop you and I would say, do not think about it, just do it". Rohini looked at her and agreed with everything she said. She was also a bit anxious about Shaan's behavior in the future if something of this sort happens between them. She had to sort it and to do this, she asked Shaan to meet her to discuss a very important issue before they agreed to marry each other.

Rohini met him and started questioning him on everything that she wanted to sort out. They did have few heated arguments, but later, things concluded, and they decided to marry each other. Rohini was satisfied and was much more in love with him. For her, love won over materialistic things. Their love was true, and they both knew it. She felt blessed and proud and her respect for Shaan had increased after this meeting. They never discussed it again. As is rightly said by William Shakespeare, "Love is blind, and lovers cannot see the pretty follies that they themselves commit".

Rohini had received many job offers and from most of those she got the call letters. She was looking for the best opportunity for her and at last, during an interview, the recruiter was so much impressed with her, that he offered her the job with a salary she could not refuse. Her first goal was conquered and now the next goal was getting married to Shaan. On the other hand, Shaan's first round of interviews were becoming his last ones. He never received a call for the second round. This was creating a tension between them. Nothing seemed to be fine in his life. He was getting panic attacks that he might lose Rohini because of not getting a job. There is a saying, "If you want something and work to achieve it, all forces work with you to achieve it", the same happened with him when finally, he got his first job. This job was not what he wanted to do, and even the salary was not even close to Rohini's which was a bit demotivating for him, but he had to accept it.

Finally, after 3 years of being together from morning till evening, it was the time for them to be together for their whole life. They were finally getting married. They bought a house together, two cars, and a decent joint account balance. Everything was joint, which made them perfect for each other. Their marriage was performed as per Hindu religion and their first night was at a 5-star hotel. For their honeymoon, they traveled to Australia and New Zealand for 10 days. That was the best time of their lives. They were in a different world all together, just like all the newlyweds.

Three years passed and with time their focus shifted from each other, to making their lives better. Rohini changed her job and got a new job. Within a few months, she has been promoted to Vice Presidentship. The promotions added to her job responsibilities, new commitments, and a huge hike in salary. She knew exactly how to create a balance between house and work and because of that she always got respect in her office and her house.

Her in-laws loved her and praise her in front of everyone they met about how well she handled all the responsibilities of a wife, a daughter-in-law, and even of a vice-president in an organization. The only thing which upsets them is that she is not ready to become a mother. Her mother-in-law would always complain "Rohini, if you want me to die in peace, please let me see the face of my grandchild. I will not ask you for anything else". Rohini averted this by saying "I want you near me always and that is the reason why I don't want to do it". Even Shaan encouraged her to concentrate on her job. They both knew that once she becomes a mother, she won't be able to work again.

Shaan's professional life had many ups and downs. He does not like his job and if he could find another one, he wouldn't stay there for a long time. He would either resign or be asked to resign within a few months of his joining. He gives many excuses, sometimes the office is not good, sometimes the boss is not good, and sometimes the location wis not good enough. Rohini gets very upset with his childish attitude towards his jobs and always said that he needs to focus and get serious with his job. They cannot survive only on her salary and Shaan's salary never increases even if he switches jobs.

Somewhere in his head, Shaan knows that Rohini is much stronger than him professionally for which he takes advantage of her. He wants to start a business, but Rohini doesn't allow since she knows that he wouldn't be able to do business. She fears losing her hard-earned savings for which she works very hard. She cannot afford it, and Shaan starts feeling that Rohini is insecure about his ideas. As per his thoughts, she would never want to see him rise above her, as she is more educated than him and the whole society looks at her as an inspiration.

Soon their differences start to surface, and, often, they argue about the same or other petty issues. He purposely fights with her, and she turns it into a very ugly fight. During their fights, her tone gets so high that a person sitting in the neighboring apartments could hear everything clearly whereas Shaan's voice during those arguments becomes like a mouse trying to keep the argument within the walls of their house. Rohini is a dominating person. She is capable of making decisions for herself, and the house, and those decisions are never wrong. Her calculation is always very precise. Whereas, Shaan is not like her. He jumps to conclusions without listening and understanding fully, which lands him into incorrect decisions or sometimes loss of money.

The friction between them is rising. The small issues have now become big issues. Shaan starts drinking whiskey heavily. He gets drunk and sleeps on the couch, or sometimes on the floor. This provokes Rohini even more. Because of such reasons, she leaves for her parent's house a couple of times, and Shaan has to bring her back after a huge offering of apologies.

After a few weeks, she finds him drunk again. Those people, for whom she is an inspiration, now start calling her and giving her advice and even say that Shaan might not like that she has reached such a level when he is on the same level where he started his career. Rohini and Shaan had discussed this before marriage and still now their marriage is in a fix. She sits for hours idly, thinking about her future with Shaan, and what will happen to her if they broke apart. She feels depressed, loses her appetite, sleep, and even the zeal to work. Shaan on the other hand takes her situation very lightly and thinking that she is faking never believes her. He curses her and blames her for her situation. He never realizes that she is sick and getting sicker and sicker by the day.

Thinking that a child would save their relationship they try many times but are unable to conceive. Her family and other known people suggest millions things to them, especially to Rohini, on what she should do to conceive. She hears everyone and even tries it all, but again there is no success. Then, her mother-in-law suggests them to go for a medical check-up. They agree to go for the medical checkup and are told that the report will be ready by the next week.

The present week went horribly, with many negative dreams coming to her mind about the report, whereas Shaan was normal as if he knew there is no problem with him, and all the problems are with Rohini. The report is with them and it states that Rohini is healthy to conceive but Shaan is not. The pregnancy report serves as the next blow to her. This means that they cannot become parents. Rohini's only way to save the relationship is also over and she is in a miserable situation.

She cannot sleep during the night and just cries, blaming Shaan that she has made a mistake by marrying him. Shaan just gives her the medicine which controls her emotion and lets her go to sleep. That's the best he can ever do for her. He never wants to argue with her as he knows that she will not understand him and eventually might hurt him or herself. He is worried about her. He knows he has become an alcoholic but never harms her physically, even though she abuses him, throws things on the floor and even runs away from the house at night. She sits in the temple and when he tries to bring her back home, she beats him and asks him not to touch her. People around are aware of her condition and help him bring her back home. Earlier she used to visit a psychologist but lately, she is in need of a psychiatrist.

Every day he wakes up in the morning, makes her tea, breakfast, and drops her at the office on his way to his work. He starts trying his best to console her. He knows that his inability to become a father has damaged her a lot and this is not under his control. He is taking medicines to boost himself up, but nothing is helping him. He wants to turn things to normal  like Rohini wants, but it is just a wishful thinking for him. He starts blaming himself for not being sincere to his profession and he is unable to accept responsibility for her mental illness.

Trying to resolve his issues with Rohini, he purchases an international package and business class tickets to a place where she can relax and enjoy herself. He wants her to have a good time. The room he has booked for themselves are a presidential room and private tours. But Rohini is still not happy and she complains about everything he does. Deep down, she wants to be happy, wants to laugh but instead, she ends up screaming and crying due to her depression. One time she yells at him in such a way that the people nearby have to call the cops thinking that he has come to harm her. He gets released only when she calms down and takes her complaint back. That becomes the breaking point for him.

As soon as they reach India, Shaan asks Rohini to leave for her house and to come back only when she is cured. All the love, affection, and responsibilities towards each other are washed away and only emptiness is what they feel

2 years ago, Shaan had a medical problem. He was in his office and suddenly started feeling uncomfortable. When his colleagues checked with him, they found out that he was burning with high fever. He was rushed to a

nearby hospital where he slipped into a coma. He was at the hospital for a month and Rohini was looking after him. His mother would come in the morning and stay there till dawn. She would leave her son once Rohini used to be back from her job. At that time Rohini was very busy at her office after she became the Vice President. Still, Rohini used to work at the office and the rest she would complete at the hospital once Shaan was asleep. In the morning, her in-laws would come to the hospital, and then she used to rush to her house to get dressed, prepare food for her mother-in-law, and then leave for her office. The same routine was followed for a month. Her dedication to him gave results and he recovered. She didn't have a bed at the hospital, and she used to sleep on the couch. Sometimes, that couch was occupied by others, so she had to sit straight and sleep. Rohini loved him a lot and did all she could do to get him back on his feet.

For Shaan, now things have gone out of his hands and he is cerebrating his future with her. He is tired of taking care of her, and handling all the bullshit she vents only on him. The best resolution is to get separated. For this, he decides to hire a divorce lawyer. His friend advocate him against her and when they hear that he was looking for a lawyer, they happily give him the contact details of a lawyer who is one of the best in the city. The next day, the lawyer carefully hears the grievances and shows his real sympathy to his client. He knows exactly what charges he needs to press against the spouse. He shows Shaan the following draft allegations, for his approval:

1.) Mentally torturing him due to her better standing- She is dominating him and making sure that he doesn't do well in life.

2.) Filled with pride– She is being supercilious.

3.) Extra-Marital Affair – She has an extramarital affair with her boss. She did get her self-promoted to become the Vice  President of the company.

4.) Unsound mind before marriage – She was of unsound mind before she got married to him.

5.) Cannot become a mother – She is barren. She deliberately kept it a secret. She always gave an irrational reason for not becoming a mother. After confirming by the test, she is now threatening to charge us for manipulating the results which are false and baseless.

Once Shaan approves the said allegations, the draft is faired and sent to his wife. The application has been drafted in a way to attract sympathy from the court and circumvent the alimony. Shaan and his parents know that the allegations mentioned in the application are untrue, but they never bother to know what repercussions it may bring. In the beginning, his parents were totally against his decision of taking a divorce from her but they have to agree after seeing that their son was very adamant about it. When they ask him to change the allegations, he bluntly refuses. For him, it is a war and, everything for him is fair in love and war. The court is to become his battlefield.

Rohini, unable to cope up with her demanding job, is feeling more and more depressed. She understands that she is alone and might not be able to overcome this disease. She is getting weaker by the day. She only wants three things – love, care, and peace. Unfortunately, these three things are nowhere near her. She wants to live the same life in which she lived with the same high spirits and enthusiasm. She is waiting to get back to her house, work, and husband to live a normal life just like others live. But something else is written in her fate. Within a week Rohini's mother and father come rushing to her house and ask her to pack the bags. When she reasons with them, they say that they want her with them for some days. They want to have a good time with her. She is happy and readily agrees. She never guesses that this might be her last time in this house.

The next day, she gets introduced to a lawyer who is going to take up her divorce case. Hearing about divorce, Rohini is surprised and horrified. She is in shock and doesn't understand why her parents want her to take a divorce from the love of her life. Her father gives her the notice sent by Shaan's lawyer. She is heartbroken. She had never imagined such a thing from him. She loved him a lot and she used to fight with him, just because she believed that their love was much higher than all the negative emotions. For the world, they were the best couple ever.

Being husband and wife, they have the right to fight with each other and say things to each other which mean nothing, just like other couples do. She doesn't have a word to say and retires to her room and locks herself inside. It takes her 2 days to get over this fact that she is getting divorced from the man she loves and wants to spend her entire life with. Her dreams are shattered and she can feel emptiness inside her body. Her feet are heavier than her bodyand she is not able to lift them as they have become as stiff as a rock. Reaching her parents she asks them, "Mom and Dad, am I such a bad person that everyone wants to leave me? I don't see a single ray of happiness in my life, is life being fair to me? Am I being fair with life? Don't you think I should end this life so that this misery that we all are suffering can get over?"

Listening to this her father asks her to sit near him and starts explaining to her, "Rohini, there is nothing like bad life, first thing. Your life is much better than those who are suffering from a very frightful disease. Still, they try to live as happily as they can. You should watch the movie, Anand, in which Rajesh Khanna says, "Hum aane waale gham ko kheench taan kar aaj ki khushi pe le aate hai… aur us khushi mein zehar ghol dete hai. ( We pull the coming sorrow and bring it to the happiness of today… and add poison in that happiness.) You need to live your life not for anyone else but for yourself. You have earned this life and you should live". Confused, but agreeing with her father, she asks her mother for some tea and her mother, wiping her tears, readily runs to prepare her some. While reading the letter again, Rohini's eyes are wide open. She looks at her father and says "Every single thing written here is a lie. Dad, how can he do this to me? I gave him everything and he gave me this depression. He is unable to become a father. Look at this line – how can he point on my character? Who permitted him? I achieved everything myself. He was a loser and he is still a loser. I swear to god I will not leave him. I will fight this case against him and will show him what I am. Dad, please call the lawyer tomorrow morning".

The date for the case arrives, and Rohini is smartly dressed. She arrives at the court with her lawyer and father. Waiting for her turn she sees Shaan standing and discussing the case with his lawyer. She wants to approach him, but her lawyer asks her to maintain distance as anything she does will go against her. Rohini stands still but her eyes are all focused on Shaan. He can see her but pretends not to. Soon, their case number is announced, and they enter the family court. The judge looks at them and says, "I don't know what the problem with the younger generation is? Why do they marry when they cannot handle themselves?" Looking at the couple and then the lawyers, he leans towards them and says, "Don't you get bored of advising the same reasons to all of your clients? Try to bring some new interesting issues. I am bored with the same topics. The same matter I read the day before yesterday." The judge asks Shaan's lawyer to file the response within a week and gives a date for the next week.

While leaving the court Shaan and Rohini stare at each other and turn towards the opposite directions leaving the premises. The lawyers are working their best to make their client win this case but also try to stretch the case so they can earn more money. The lawyers are charging per hearing, so more hearings will mean more earnings. For them, they are their clients, and this is justified as this is their livelihood. Shaan's lawyer asks him to skip the date as he was busy with another case. And on the next date, Rohini's lawyer is unavailable for the hearing. On both, the hearings their juniors are visiting, which makes them charge for those dates.

Meanwhile, Rohini's father develops sugar and high blood pressure because of his daughter's future, as to how is she going to live, and will she be able to see her family again. The same is with Shaan's family. They are as concerned for their son as Rohini's parents. They don't know what to do or what more is written in their fate. They are not that rich, so every penny spent on the lawyers is pinching them. Though their son is spending, they very well knew the importance of money. Money saved, is money earned!

Days after days and months after months have passed, but the fight is still on. Sometimes the lawyers are unavailable and sometimes the judge is on a holiday. During these dates three times, the judge is changed. The lawyers are trying to turn this fight uglier so they can mint more money out, and they are encouraged by their clients. Rohini's lawyer files a police complaint against Shaan and he gets arrested. The worst thing is that the court is closed for 3 days meaning that he will stay in jail till then. Three days after submitting a bond in court, Shaan's bail is accepted. This creates more friction between them and now Shaan is discussing with his lawyer how he can harm her legally. "Unfortunately, in India, a girl's complaint is heard faster than a men's. It will be better for you to do nothing and be as safe as you can".

Sitting at home Rohini remembers her conversation with Shaan's mother before her marriage when she had warned her, "Beta, this is something you have to decide. You are well educated and much smarter than

Shaan. You know you will get a better job, better pay, and better opportunities in life. My son may not be as successful as you are, and this may be the bitter part. A male cannot see his wife doing better than him because this is a male-dominated society and those who are unable to do so are looked at as inferior. If you both can handle this, then you can go ahead with it". Rohini has tears in her eyes while thinking about all that.

One year has passed and the case is still in court. Judges are changing frequently but the lawyers are still the same with the same intentions and dedications. Shaan's life has become a roller coaster as nothing is going well. He is still struggling with his jobs, his father has passed away due to a heart attack and his mother is suffering from cancer. On the other hand, Rohini's life is full of enthusiasm. She has entered into a relationship with a man who is working in the same office, and she is now waiting for her divorce to finalize. Once separated, she is going to get married with her new love. She has changed her address as she shifts to Mumbai where she is working now. She was enjoying this new life, induced with confidence, and interest which were missing earlier. Depression was the toughest war she is still battling, but now that is also diminishing with time.

Shaan arrives at the court and finds Rohini with her lawyer. He was seeing her after so long as her lawyer usually comes alone. Today was the final judgment day when the judge will validate their separation. Seeing her made his heart feel for her again. Wearing a top and pair of jeans, he could see a change in her attitude. The last time when he saw her, she was wearing a salwar-kurta, ponytail and her complexion was terrible. She had grown darker, her eyes had dark circles, and she had gained a lot of weight. Today, however, he could see a much smarter Rohini, just the same way she was before marrying him. She has grown much fairer, her hair are now straighter where they were wavy once, her eyes have that brightness which he loved the most in her and he was now much slimmer than she was before even before she met him the first time in the theater. His affection for her is filling his heart and making him feel guilty for whatever he did to her and for leaving her. He wants to reach her and re-start a new life with her. Without thinking much, he goes up to her and with confidence he tries to have a conversation with her, asking how she is and where she had been all this time.

Knowing that she will be upset he delivers her the sad news of his father's death and on his mother's medical condition. Rohini is listening to everything but doesn't react, neither asks about his health or how he has been. After dragging the conversation, he realizes that Rohini is not interested in talking to him. With an exasperated expression, he leaves and sits near his lawyer. Looking at the lawyer and then to her while she was talking and giggling with her own lawyer he says, "Look at her attitude, she has changed so much. She has forgotten all the good things I did for her. She didn't even react after listening about my parents. She is to be blamed for all that has happened to me and my family. How can she be so manipulative and cold-hearted?" The lawyer quietly listens to him but says nothing.

Their case number is announced, and they are asked to appear before the judge. The very first judge was at the chair and while looking at the case file and then looking at the couple he smiles and says you are still fighting for your divorce?" He starts reading their file again. After closing the file, he looks at the couple and says, "if you still don't want to live with each other, you should accept and move ahead in life. Children, whatever issues you have might be reconcilable just try again!" Shaan looks over at Rohini who was not looking at him but instead at the judge. She raises her hand and says, "Judge, I have suffered a lot with him but not anymore, I want to break free from this meaningless relationship which has nothing but misery. The life I have lived before was painful and depressing. The life I am living today is much happier and making me fall in love all over again, which I had given up before. I request you to please break me free from this". The judge looks at Shaan while removing his glasses and asks him, "Do you also want to break free from this?" Shaan looks at

Rohini but still she does not look at him. With anger he nods his head and asks the judge to confirm their divorce. The judge, wearing back his glasses, signs the documents and pronounces that from today they are free from their marriage.

Signing the document, Shaan looks at Rohini one last time and says, "From today I am setting you free. I wish you all the best for your future life and am always there for you whenever you are in need of a true friend". Rohini, without looking at him, signs the document, turns towards her lawyer and leaves the courtroom.

# Retreat

Standing at the immigration line, waiting for the border security agent to let me enter into this country, I am tired and want some fresh air to breathe. No one knows me here and there is no one to control me. As the immigration lines move inch by inch the memory of my past is knocking my head, trying to enter and spoil my present. I must lock it and never let it in.

By occupation, I am an actor, though not as famous as the known one, but famous for the projects I have done. My name is Raman Dua. I am from a small town near Shimla. I ran away from my house to become an actor. At that time, I was confident that I will compete with those A+ actors, but never understood the dedication and perseverance they have put in to uphold this position.

Born and brought up in a Gharwal family, I have lived on the hills of Himachal Pradesh. Living in a mansion with many servants running around the house, we never had to pour even a glass of water as everything used to be prepared and served by them in utensils made of silver. They themselves always used Banana leaves as plates and for drinking water they drank from clay pots. My grandfather Late Sukhiram, the head of the panchayat of our village. He was a wrestler and had won many medals in wrestling tournaments in India and abroad. He was the most influential man in the village and the same went as lineage to my father.

My father, Ram Kishore, is also a wrestler but not as famous as my grandfather. My father only wrestled because his father wanted him to. My father was a very good speaker and used to resolve major issues of the villagers within a few minutes. Because of this, he was elected as the Sarpanch and was the most influential man in the village. He completed his education from the UK and used to wear designer clothes. His dressing sense was much loved that every day his picture in new clothes were printed in the papers. He used to smoke a pipe and drank the most expensive scotch, which his friends used to bring whenever they met him  every other day.

Almost all the villagers used to work for us. Some were farming in our lands, some in shops or other businesses which we had.  All decisions about the village or the villagers were taken by my father. My mother's name is Dr. Shruti. She also has completed her education and PhD in the UK. Even though she was very much educated she chose to be a housewife just to make sure that I was not neglected. Her father was a freedom fighter.

 Snow-laden mountains glistened under the golden sun rays, and the vision brightened up our mornings each day. Densely populated trees and other flora and fauna were living with us. Our school was in the same village, and our father hired English speaking teachers from the town to teach us in our village. I was a backbencher and cavalier about my classes, and quite frequently skipped the classes which led me to get lower marks in the exams. I was good at sports and was very good looking compared to the other boys in the school and my neighbourhood. My parents, however, had a different opinion. They were just concerned about my education and nothing else. For them, I was average in everything and told me to only concentrate on studies as good looks  will not help in making a life. For me, they were no less than villains.

Despite of our status in the village, my father never asked me not to play with other boys. All the other boys were my friends, and all the mischievous activities were done together. My status was never a hindrance for my friends, and we used to play without any limitations. In our group, we were about 15 kids and all of us loved playing cricket. I loved playing football, but my friends never knew this game, and I never forced them to learn how to play. Whenever we used to play a cricket match with the other village boys, I was the only one who had all the accessories required for this game. The other kids never liked it as they didn't have it all. I never used to flaunt, but they used to think I was, just because I could afford to have all those accessories. Whenever we played, I felt that they used to play a bit aggressively with me, just to satisfy their jealousy.

As we grew older my friend circle reduced to only two close friends. This was because with age our priorities differed, and our status was more defined. The 2 friends were not as rich as I was but were different from the rest. At this age, I used to choose my friends based on their status and not how friendly they were with me. I understood that education was not my forte still, I enrolled myself in MBA studies. I never wanted to pursue MBA, but my parents did. I wanted to become an actor. Going to the gymnasium, and partying with friends were the only things I loved to do. The gymnasium was in our village, and this was gifted to me by my uncle living in Mumbai. My uncle who was my mother's younger brother, was also very educated and was the owner of a very big IT company. Recently he suffered a big loss due to which he had lost almost everything, including his wife and kid who left him. As he was living in Mumbai, he had good connections with Bollywood actors, directors and producers. I always used to get excited whenever he visited us as he used to tell me stories about his friends who were actors.

Since childhood, movies and Bollywood used to attract me very much. Watching movies, dancing to songs, and mimicking the dialogues always amused me. It was the only thing that made me happy. At school, I used to get the best actor awards and I always wanted to work in Bollywood as an actor. I had the perfect body, was good at dialog delivery, and danced quite well. Still my family was against me on becoming an actor. As per them, becoming an actor was not an easy thing. Many people go to Mumbai to become an actor, but only one reaches the top. I knew it but I also knew that I could reach to that level on the top. MBA was not helping me to reach anywhere near acting and that was bothering me. I had to do something to get to my goal- Mumbai.

During the same time, my uncle from Mumbai came to visit us, and as usual he started telling me about his meeting with some Bollywood actors. I asked him if I could become an actor and  he said, "If you have that ability and that factor that actors need to have, then yes, you can become an actor. But also know that their life is not at all easy. It looks very vibrant but in reality, it's not". I was partially convinced as I knew my parents might have asked him to demoralize me on this, still, he was not the villain, but my parents were. I wanted to break away from my village and prove to the whole world, and especially my parents that I could do it. I started to think about shifting to Mumbai but knew that my parents would never agree to help me financially with this. I called my uncle who lived in Mumbai. It was very heart-breaking to hear that he was also not willing to help or do anything against my parents' will. He used to get financial help from my father and that is why he couldn't go against them, though I never saw or heard any financial transactions between them, but I believed so.

After knowing that no one will help me, I decided to run away from there. A day earlier to my escape, I withdrew all my money from my savings account which was enough for me to survive in Mumbai for at least for 6 months. I pretended that I was going to college, and then waited for five beats before turning back to my house. Many servants were there at home and I knew someone would see me, so I planned that I will go back home and behave like I had forgotten my book. At home, I removed the books and packed my clothes, had some milk, and packed everything I could. While exiting one of the servants noticed me and asked the reason for my return. Hurriedly, I told them that I had forgotten my book and for that had to return. I knew if I wasted more time there my mother might catch me, and ask one of the servants to drop me to college. To avoid being seen by the villagers I was pumping my knees and arms to run faster through the thick hilly jungles so I could reach the bus faster and avoid any interference in between.

Finally, I reached and boarded the bus wearing a cap, so no one could see me. While riding towards the city, I knew that going forward I won't be able to live the life I had been living till now, no one will do my work, cook me food and even fold my clothes. I will have to do it by myself. But I was going to live a thrilling life with my new expedition. I was waiting to reach Mumbai and becoming a successful actor. My parents, who would be worried about my whereabouts, might be calling my friends to get hold of me and finally will lodge a missing complaint at the police station. They will be very worried and annoyed once they find my letter which I wrote to tell them where I am now. I was deep in thinking when the sudden break by the driver broke my train of thoughts.

The railway station was in front of me. I hurriedly ran towards the booking counter and purchased a ticket for Mumbai. As per my plan, the train should leave within 2 hours. But reaching at the station, an announcement was flashing that this train was delayed by 4 hours. I knew I cannot wait much as my father will soon be here and catch hold of me. So, I ran towards the train leaving the platform. I didn't know where this train was going. It was leaving for Delhi as per a co-passenger. On the train, the TT (Travelling Ticket Examiner) was examining the passenger's tickets and soon he demanded my ticket. I gave him the ticket which I had purchased for my rail travel to Mumbai to examine, to which he raised an alarm that I have boarded the wrong train and took me to the railway police station at the next railway station, where the train halted for couple of hours. I managed to explain to the police officer, and he let me continue my journey to Delhi.

The following day, I reached New Delhi railway station, and I took a taxi to leave for the Domestic Airport to catch my flight to Mumbai. This was not the first time I had come to the airport, last month along with my parents we had gone to Milan to see the Milan Fashion week, but I had never travelled domestically in India. I checked-in at the counter of the airline and bought myself a ticket to Mumbai. I only had a handbag which I carried on my shoulder to the plane. Within 2 hours I was in Mumbai. Coming out of the airport I was thrilled and excited. Finally, I had reached my destination. Now nothing could stop me from becoming an actor. I hired a taxi and asked the driver to drive me to Bandra. I knew this was the place where some prominent film production houses are. Checked -into a hotel and waited eagerly for the sun to fall asleep, so the moon can take the charge and let me have a good night. I knew the next morning I was going to get my acting kick started and within a few weeks I would be very famous, and my parents would feel proud of me. In my sleep, I was able to see myself walking with celebrities all around and people were shouting my name and asking for my autograph.

Being indolent by nature, I woke up in the afternoon, and by the time I left the room it was the time when the shutters were dropping down, as the working day for everyone was coming to an end. Leaving the hotel premises, I hired a taxi to one of the production houses to discuss if they could take me in a film. I could see a line outside the production house and reaching there I was asked to stand in the queue. The queue was a long one, and I could only see the heads one after another in a straight line. I went to the guard and asked him to let me in, but it seemed that he was too busy instructing others to form a line. I had never felt like this before, never stood in a line and no one ever spoke rudely or ignored me this way. Angrily, I ordered him to open the gate for me and he in the same manner asked me to be in the line. The level of his behaviour enraged me. I couldn't bear him any longer and I chose to go back.

While sitting in a taxi and going back to the hotel, a conversation started between me and the driver. He said that he also had come to this city to become an actor but never got a chance. I knew why he didn't, as he was not at all a star material. He was not handsome, nor had a good built, his hair was thin, and he was overweight. Finding me staring at him he said, "Don't go on my structure now, I used to be as handsome as you are when I came here, but the struggle to survive here is so much that I had to opt for this job". I looked at him and said, "Well, this is your story but mine is different. I came here to become a star and see within few months you will see me in films, take my autograph or else you will have to stand in line to have one." I spoke with pride with my head held high. The driver looked at me from the rear-view mirror with a frown. We reached the hotel and while I was giving him the money he said, "I don't know why you think that getting into films is very easy. Some people have wasted their whole life to find a single role and you think it's like plucking an orange from an orchard? If yes, then get ready to waste your life here, but if possible, go back from where you have come". I looked at him, took the change and left for my room. I knew he was a loser, and for a loser the whole world looks like the paradise of losers.

Soon, after repeated humiliation by the guards at the gates of production houses, my determination and morale got depleted. It's been three months here but still I was sitting in the hotel room doing nothing. I had no friends and no other place to go so I started feeling depressed. I desperately needed a friend with whom I could speak. I couldn't sleep at night and all I used to do was cry my heart out and then thinking about how to ask for forgiveness from my parents. Nothing seemed to be going right for me, I had thought. I realised that I had to do something or I would run out of cash. I started thinking about my future, what disasters my fate beholds. Becoming an actor was now far from reality. In the room, I just was eating, sleeping, and repeating the same. My body was becoming flabby and I couldn't do anything about this.

One night while watching a movie, I was not feeling good, I felt like something is missing within me, this is not who I am, and I cannot be slave of depression. I stood up and started making myself a to-do list. I prepared a timetable which I will have to follow without fail. The first target was to go to the gym in the morning and start a disciplined life routine. The second target was to get a job to sustain in this big and heartless city. Third thing was to start finding auditions to achieve the real reason for coming here.

The gym in the hotel was well equipped, but had less machines due to limited space. To start the exercise, I broke 7 days into different exercises and Sunday as a rest day. Mondays I did the chest workouts. Seven exercises for the chest with 12 reps each. Every workout needed to be in ascending order. Tuesdays were for back and abs. 4 -5 exercises with 12 reps. Wednesdays were shoulders and abs. Thursdays, arms again, Fridays were for legs and lastly, Saturdays only cardio.

The second thing was getting a job. This was tough for me. I never expected that I would ever ask anyone for a job apart from working in movies. In my hometown, we used to give jobs to others and here I was asking for one. I didn't have my certificates as I was never prepared for this. I searched for many jobs, but no one took me because I didn't have my certificates. I had practically gone to all offices around my hotel but failed to get even one. After getting rejected by almost all offices, the focus shifted to restaurants and other stores. My luck in getting jobs seemed to be not with me! While walking on the street of Bandra, I was stressed about my job. The money which I had brought was mostly spent in a much higher pace than I had thought. One day, I found a door where it was written 'Vacancy available'. I looked at the board and it was a restaurant. "I think they require a manager. Okay, I can do this", thinking this, I walked in and went to the person in charge of this position. After a brief interaction, he said that the position which was available in the restaurant was for a dishwasher. Hearing this I stood up and started walking out. I couldn't believe what I had heard and didn't want to speak about it any further!

The next day I started my job hunt again. "I will never do a blue-collar job that is for sure, only white-collar". I thought to myself while exiting the hotel. Going around searching for a job was just like searching for God to me. I didn't know what was going to happen next in my life. Walking towards the end of the busy street, I saw a board on which it was written, Salesperson required'. I was happy, and I ran towards it. I entered the shop and that shop was for kid's toys. The owner was a sikh and was a bit aged. I went to him and after a brief interview, he hired me. I was happy, very happy! I wanted to share this news, but I didn't have anyone. In the night I was lying on the bed and started talking to the ceiling fan. I told the ceiling fan how happy I was about getting the job and asked my pillow to wake me up early the day after since it was my first day for my job. The pillow obeyed me and woke me up early in the morning. I rushed to the shop and started my first day. Selling a toy is a tough job as compared to buying it! I had to convince a customer to buy a 100 Rupee toy, whereas there were more spectators than buyers. My second thing as per my to-do list was achieved.

Money in my pocket, I was no more under pressure for spending it wisely. Now, I had to focus on the third thing on my to-do list. I needed to find auditions. Before that, I had to create my portfolio, as I read this in one of the film magazines. Searching for the right person was a pain. The best were extremely expensive, and the rest were not worth it. "The salary from this job was not enough. I had to find an alternate job or an additional job. I need to hire a better photographer and for that, they charged a fortune", I thought. My muscles were very good, and I looked strong. I got a job as a bouncer at a pub where I had to report from 7 pm till 3 in the morning. Timings suited me as it was not overlapping with my first job which ended at 6 pm. At the pub, my job was to look for any mischievous activities. Every night there was one or another drunken person getting beaten or thrown out of the pub by me. Everyone at the pub used to like me and soon I had many friends. The emptiness within me was now being fulfilled. Health consciousness made me stay away from alcohol and cigarettes, and that was what the owners of the pub liked in me. I started living a frugal life to cut on my expenses just to hire a professional photographer who would create my portfolio. And soon that day arrived. I had enough money to hire one. He prepared me a portfolio and now I could send it to all production houses. Submitting at every house, I was now waiting for them to call me. I was doing my morning job at the toy store and evening at the pub. It was a very painful task for me to bear.

One evening during my shift in the pub, there was a person who was staring gawkily at me. His hair was curly, tan complexion, a bit fat but was tall. At first, I tried to ignore him but then I had to go to him and ask the reason for staring at me. "You don't deserve working here as a bouncer. You should try in movies" he said while looking at me from head to toe. "There is that x-factor in you which separates you from others." While saying this he handed over a visiting card to me and asked me to meet the undersigned person. On asking him his name, he smiled and said, "Ask the same question to the person you will meet tomorrow". The next morning, I requested leave from the toy store and went to the address printed on the visiting card. Reaching the venue, I found out that it was a corporate building. Going towards the elevator, I checked the floor again, and pressed the button on that floor. I reached the 11th floor. The building was made of clear glass. It was so clear that it felt like there were no walls. That was a production house, and when I showed the card to the guard, with respect he asked me to enter the office without waiting hours in that line where others were standing and waiting for their turn. I entered the office and asked for Rakesh, the name mentioned on the card. The receptionist showed me his desk and I went there.

Rakesh was a dark man, wore big black spectacles and his hair were glued to his head with excessive oil. As I handed him the card, he looked at me from top to bottom, and then asked me to submit my portfolio.

He then asked me to wait for him to come back. He took my portfolio and the card which I handed over to him, and went inside a big cabin. After sometime, he returned with a paper. It was an agreement. He asked me to read the agreement and then to sign it. Reading the agreement, it stated that this production house is hiring me, and I will have to work with them on every project or character they will offer me. The locking period of this agreement was for 5 years and I was prohibited from working with any other production house till this agreement was in place. I agreed and signed the contract. I asked Rakesh about the person whom I had met at the bar and gave me his reference. He said that he was the owner of this agency and his name was Ram Prakash Kumar. I had heard and seen him before on TV, but meeting in person was always different and sometimes you don't recognise on the spot. I wanted to meet him, but he was not available.

Now, my third to-do list was complete, and my reason to come to Mumbai was also achieved. Soon, I started shooting for a daily soap and was becoming quite famous. During this one year of struggle, there was not a single day when I did not think of my parents, but the guilt of running away from them stopped me from meeting them. I knew I cannot face them. But it was also true that because of them I took this decision and had to see this hardship.

Months passed and I bought a house for myself, 3 imported cars, and even had a manager. I asked my manager to arrange a trip to my hometown. Due to work pressure, I had only three days in hand. There was no airport in my hometown and any mode of transportation would take at least 12 hours to reach there. My manager hired a helicopter for me, and all clearance was taken to land at my hometown. On landing, I could see a huge gathering of people to greet me. There was local police who cleared my way to reach the house. My parents were not informed about my visit and that made me more anxious. The fear of meeting them, and the fear to see my parents cry meeting me after a long time was freezing my blood. Reaching home, I ran inside just like I used to do when I used to come from school. I could see all the old servants bowing down at me with their hands folded just the same way they used to do when I was a kid. But neither my father nor my mother came to meet me. They were not alive anymore. My mother had passed away with the shock of my running away from the house, and my father had passed away just a year ago. My uncle who lived in Mumbai had shifted here and was now looking after this property.

Meeting my uncle, I knew that now he must have taken over this property and he would never let me take the inheritance which legally belonged to me. He was very happy seeing me, and walked towards me spreading his arms to hug me. He was bluffing. I knew that sometime later he would show me his real colours. He asked me to enter the house and while entering, looking at the couches and side tables, a flashback was running through my eyes. The rooms where the guests would wait for my father was still the same and the staircase was still cemented with wooden railings which used to make a sound as we pressed against it with pressure. Walking down the corridor was a courtyard that still had that cot where my mother used to sit, and a servant used to apply oil on her hair and next to it was a cane seat and a hookah placed near it. A table with a drawer was placed nearby too which had the tobacco that my father and my grandfather used to smoke. These memories were running through my eyes in the form of tears. I knew this will be the last time I was going to see all these things and yes I should be punished as I never cared about anyone but just me. I could hear my mother crying while taking my name and my father trying to console her and giving her false hopes that soon, I would come back. But I never came back to wipe her tears, hug her in my arms and say that her son would be with her always. I never came to my father and held his hand the same way I used to, when as a kid I walked with him. They made a mistake in bringing me to life and for this they deserve to die like this, they made me run away from here, and in return, they died without having their only son with them by their side.

I was crying like a small child throwing my hands in the air and shouting their names. My uncle held my arms and took me into the room. "Beta, your parents waited for you endlessly. Everyday your mother would call me and ask if I had met you. Your father searched for you and followed your steps. He came to know that you went to Delhi and from there you flew to Mumbai. He went to Mumbai and we all searched for you. He wanted to help you in becoming an actor, but we couldn't trace you. Before his death, he wrote his will". He handed me the will and when I opened it, I could read that all the property was in my name and my uncle was the keeper till I don't claim it. I looked at him and he had tears in his eyes. "Today my promise that I made to your mother and father has been fulfilled. This is your property now you take care of this and let me go back". I had no words for him and hugged him and went into my room where I used to sleep. My room was just the same way as it used to be.

I did not stay there overnight, but instead decided to return. On the way back, I was thinking about the time that I had spent there. My whole life in that house was going through my eyes like a picture. My parents were alive and I was the same young kid who was running around the house with my own mischief. Comparing my life, if I would have been staying with them instead of staying alone in Mumbai, it was sure that I wouldn't have become what I am today. I knew I would never come back and live in that house. I would either sell this property or will lease it out, and will soon decide on this.

While shooting, I met with an accident and was bed ridden. Alone, the memory of my parents was killing me. I could hear their voices all around me, and whenever I closed my eyes, would see them staring at me. I was getting disturbed, I was getting sick and weak, I was slipping into depression. The death of my parents was making me feel guilty that I had killed them, but I never got the time to sit and think about it.

Three years passed after my parents' death and nothing changed for me. Busy work schedules and no time to think what next I should do in my life. I didn't laugh, nor speak to my friends much. I feared sitting alone or doing anything that gave me pleasure. The depression was stopping me from doing things I liked. I used to wake up in the middle of the nights and start crying without a reason. I was still not seeing a doctor as I was afraid of hospitals, doctors, and medicines.

Miland, a good friend of mine, arranged for a psychologist, and soon my treatment started. The first day of our session went well. Dr. Sanjana who was a well-known psychologist aged somewhere near to mine was treating me. She was a very attractive female, fair lady with gorgeous figure. I lost my senses the moment I met her. She asked me to come twice a week and then she would  reduce the visits to once a week if she found improvements. With her I used to feel secure, I wanted to meet her every day and even called her many times in the pretext of having difficulties or coming up with some stupid or weird questions. Those sessions were helping me, I could feel that the burden on my head and shoulders were reducing and I was getting relaxed. It was all going well between us. At least that's what I thought! I started developing feelings for her and I guess she knew it but never reacted. Soon, she left the clinic and I was left on my own. She even changed her number.

The production house with which I had signed the contract, were very controlling. They were always after me about how I must react, behave, or even what to say was all advised by them. I sometimes felt very suffocated, but I couldn't do much about it. I had to obey them and go as per the rules laid by them. Soon, the pain of working with them was going to be over. The contract tenure was coming to an end. But on refusing to extend the contract, the production house started to threaten me that they will remove me from all their projects and they eventually started doing that. Within a month I lost 2 upcoming projects and got replaced from one project. I could feel the encumbrance. Heretofore, the expenses were manageable, but now life started to become onerous.

Life was treating me the way it shouldn't. Thinking about the proverb "You reap what you sow", was coming true to me. I left my parents because of which they lost their lives, and now I am losing my work and confidence. Either I sell off the properties or agree to extend the agreement, both ways I was at loss. With 2 roads ahead and both going to hell, I chose not to take either. I was going out of this place,  shut my head to recover from this bewilderment.

# The Foster

"Ladies and gentlemen, please fasten your seatbelts. We are about to take off", announces the airhostess. I look at my wife and my 2-year-old kid and say, "Finally we are going to start the life we have been dreaming about for years". My wife looks at me, rests her head over my shoulder while my kid is busy looking outside through the windshield at the dazzling lights at the bay. Suddenly we feel a jerk. Pushback starts and with it a new chapter of our life begins.

Professionally, I am a surgeon, and an orphan. My parents were doctors. My father was a well-known urologist and my mother was a gynecologist. My parents died when I was 5 years old. My uncle didn't want to raise me, so he sent me off to an orphanage where I lived a miserable life, begging for a living. Uncle was lame because of his surgery that took place last year after he was beaten up by some goons for money that he owed to others. His presence was never liked by my parents, but he often used to visit us. He was lanky and bald with 2 strands of hair towards his forehead making it look like two horns. Huge and big mustaches that Whenever he drank anything, they also used to have a sip of that. The funny thing in him was his voice, he had a very thin voice just like a girl whose throat was sore due to having ice. My parents had a house and a lot of money which my uncle took possession of and left me impoverished. So, while my uncle was enjoying my wealth, the owner of the orphanage used to force us to beg on streets where people walking by used to give us money. If for some reason we couldn't get enough money each day from begging, the owner used to punish us by denying us food. Days were painful and nights were sleepless. Me and the others, we all feared him. None of us liked this work but because he used to beat us like animals, we were scared not to do it. There were many other kids, some were orphans abandoned like me while some were kidnapped. We all loved playing and at the end of each day of begging, we used to come back and play together. The owner had long hair and a very dark complexion and bushy eyebrows. He always used to wear bangles and wear shirts and pants. According to him, he had a soul of a female caged inside a man's body. His teeth were very dirty, and it seemed that he never had a bath. He used to stink like a pig and whenever he opened his mouth it smelled like rotten eggs. He was an alcoholic and after having a quarter would start beating and sometime sexually abuse the children, luckily, he never touched me but had beaten me a lot of times. He used to stammer a lot and because of this, his five-minute sentence used to take at least 15 minutes which was very annoying not only for us but also for his employees.

There was a boy among us whose name was Subhash. He was exceedingly good at singing. When he sang, it seemed as if time had halted. He had a great sense of humor with the perfect timing of expressions, and he also used to mimic others living with us very well. His stand-alone attitude and outstanding skills made him the brightest beggar amongst us. He used to earn much more than most of us every day. One-night Subhash disappeared. Nobody knew his whereabouts or whether he was even alive! After about a month, he came back but he behaved very differently. The owner thought that if he made Subhash more miserable, he could earn much more. So, he blinded him and broke his left leg. While he continued to earn well with his beautiful voice, the broken leg ensured that it got him more money due to people's sympathy and he couldn't run away again.

I was the only one who was extremely keen to learn. I wanted to study enough to be able to leave this filthy area. The place I used to beg was near a school. The students in the school used to study in open, so I always used to stand there to be able to learn with them.  And with my persistence I was able to listen and learn the English alphabets.

An old person who used to polish boots near that school, his name was Kapur and was about 65 years old. His son threw him and his wife outside of his house because of their old age. As per his son, he is now a burden and his presence was bothering his personal life. Whenever he used to narrate his story, both of us used to cry. I used to miss my parents and he used to miss his son's childhood. When he and his wife raised him, his son used to think his father was a hero, but, today when he has grown up, his own parents are looked upon as a burden. They have a grandson, but they are not allowed to meet him. as per their son and his wife, meeting his grandparents is a sheer waste of time. The house where his son is living was a 5 room centrally airconditioned bungalow which was owned by Kapur, and today he is living in a small house which doesn't even have a fan because there is no electricity.

He always had a soft corner for me and one day he suggested me to run far away from the orphanage and never return. He said" If you want to study further and live freely, you will have to cut yourself loose from this orphanage". He planned everything for my escape and on the decided day, he took me to the railway station where he handed me a train ticket and some money. He told me that he had informed a man in Mumbai who was going to meet me at the station and take me to a house where I was going to live. While I was boarding the train, the old man said "Beta, may God bless you. I wish you the best for your future". After my parents' death, it was the first time someone had hugged and kissed me with love. I was crying.

The journey went smoothly and when my destination came, I disembarked the train and met the person who had come to receive me. His name was Rakesh and he had a good physique. He was wearing a shirt and a pant. The shirt was not tucked and he was wearing floaters whose sole was coming out from the front. He compared my face with the picture on his mobile, looked at me and asked, "Is your name Rohan?". OR! "Yes, my name is Rohan. Who are you?", I enquired. He gave his introduction and asked me to follow him to a mansion nearby. A lady opened the door and asked us to enter the house. After a discussion with that lady, Rakesh turned towards me and said "Rohan, from now you will live here. You will do whatever they ask you to do and in return, they will educate you. Don't make them feel sorry for letting you stay here. This is the time when you can make your future." I was still afraid of one thing and ended up asking, "Are they going to make me beg on the streets?" The lady smiled and said, "No Rohan, you will stay with us and you will do the house chores. In return, we will not pay you anything but will educate you and help you become a better person".

I happily agreed. The house had many rooms and only a couple used to live in it. They didn't have children. They asked about me, what were my parents doing, why did my uncle send me to the orphanage and what sort of tortures that owner used to do to us and other kids. When I told them about my friend Subhash, their eyes had become wet. After my brief introduction, they introduced themselves to me. They were husband and wife; husband's name was Ashok and his wife's name was Roshni. In respect I used to call them as "Sir" and "Madam". I used to do all the domestic work of the house and in the afternoon the lady used to teach me. They soon started loving me as their own child. They bought me new clothes and books to read. I was very happy and felt secured with them. The man was a retired army officer with a great sense of humor and he always talked sense. Always wore a gown, golf cap and smoked a pipe. I never heard him indulging in any loose talk. Madam, was a housewife, wore simple saree and a gold bangle on her wrist. Speaking to her always gave a motherly touch.

I was about 6 or 7 years when I was brought here to their house. I couldn't trust them as all the people who

I met before were appalling, but soon I started trusting them. It has been 3 years here and now I am 10 years old. They enrolled me in 3rd standard in an English medium public school. They did not legally adopt me but took care of me just like their own child. They wrote their names as my guardian in this school. They knew that I was sharp child and wanted me to learn, they asked me to only study hard, they even hired a full-time maid to work at the house, so I was not disturbed. In every examination, I used to top. I was even awarded a scholarship from the school. I had everything I dreamt to have in my life, but I was also very afraid. In sleep, I used to wake up with chills whenever I used to dream about my uncle and the owner of the orphanage. Many times, I dreamt that the owner made me like Subhash. I used to cry with fear.

Madam was a very nice lady but with a very short temper. On some occasions she would be so angry at me that while scolding me, she would say "Rohan if you don't mend yourself, then I shall send you back from where you have come from. That man will make you beg and then you will regret for not listening to me". When she cooled down, she would call me, and while hugging she would say "Beta, don't feel bad about what I had said I was angry with you. Had you listened to me I wouldn't have been so upset with you. You know I am short tempered and when I angry, then nobody can stop me at that time. But above everything, I love you unconditionally, and I am sure you know it". Her husband would interrupt with a smile "sometimes your aunty would threaten me the same way! So, don't worry, you are not the only one with whom she behaves like this, get used to it now kid!!". All of us would laugh and proceed with our daily routine as any other family behaves. But deep down her words used to haunt me, the fear of going back would scare me from within. Even though I knew she never meant a word, my memories were so bitter that it used to come back to me.

Years passed, and today is the day of my result for + 2 class examinations. I couldn't sleep the whole night and wake up early in the morning with nervousness. Though I knew that I had done all my exams well and I might top, still I was nervous. Negative thoughts kept coming into my head. In one thought I did not score well at all, Sir and madam are very upset with me and said, "We invested so much on you, but you failed to make us proud. You bowed our heads down and failed to do anything for us. Get out of our house and never come back". I pleaded not to do so, but they handed me over to the owner, and he hurts me worse than Subhash. The next thought was, I have topped, and my parents are overjoyed. Suddenly the owner enters the house, and takes me away from them and hurts me just like Subhash. While these wild thoughts were on my mind, Sir enters the room and asks if I have checked the result online. I went to the other room and switched on the computer. The portal was loading very slowly, which might be due to heavy load or slow internet connection. A few times I had to close the portal and reopen, Sir even asked me to restart the computer.

After several efforts, finally it worked and prompted me to enter my enrolment number. While entering the number my heart was pounding very strongly. I was praying silently and then my result flashed on the screen. I could feel sweat drops dripping on my hand. Looking up I saw Sir weeping with tears of joy. He looked extremely happy and proud. He said, "Rohan, you did it my boy!" He kissed my forehead and called Madam and continued, "I know you are a diamond. You are the best of all boys around here. There is not even a single person who had ever said negative thing about you". By then Madam entered the room. Looking at Sir weeping, in concern she asked, "What happened? Why are you weeping? Is everything okay?". He smiled and asked her to look at the computer screen. Upon looking at the screen she too jumped with happiness. "You are my hero, come here give me a hug. My boy, you did it," she exclaimed in happiness while spreading her arms toward me. "You are number one, not only in your school or locality but in the whole state". Looking at Sir she continued, "Bring the best sweets in town and get it distributed in the whole neighbourhood". In some time, many reporters arrived outside our house to report that I had topped all over the state! They were waiting outside my house to take my interviews. Soon, another news  came that the state had announced to award me a cash reward for my performance in the examinations.  Getting this news, Sir and Madam  felt very proud. They looked at me and said, "You have made us very proud today Rohan. We always knew that you will rise above all and make yourself and us proud and happy". Touching their feet, I replied, "Whatever I have achieved is because of you both. If you had not accepted me, I would be on the same street with the same owner, begging. He might have broken my bones or have done anything else to make me earn more money for him. I lost my parents, but God sent you to me as my own parents". I started crying and so did they. "Rohan, please accept us as your parents. We did everything for you, we love you as our own son.  And from now on you will not call us Madam and Sir. I am your mother and he is your father. Together we are a family".

I was very happy, and I started crying more. I applied to a medical college based in Delhi and got the admission. My parents were feeling bad because I was leaving them yet felt very happy that I had gotten what I wanted. I had requested for hostel facility and the same had been accepted and provided to me. My parents bought me a flight ticket and asked me to be safe and healthy while staying there alone. While on the plane, I was thinking about my life, how it passed from bad moments to very good moments. Everything was going well so far in my life, and I was remembering and thanking that old man who bought me the train ticket, Sir and madam, who gave me a wonderful life which wouldn't be there without them.

Years passed in the blink of an eye. Today I am graduating from college and will be called a Doctor. I have become a surgeon. I did an internship in a renowned hospital and soon they appointed me. My first surgery went well. Soon, I understood that becoming a surgeon is not an easy job. It is full of risks and responsibilities. But when I see a smile on my patient's face, it is the best moment, and I feel proud of the profession that I have chosen. One day I got a patient who needed an urgent surgery. His condition was deteriorating, and I had to rush for it. The surgery started and in the operation theatre, the patient's condition started to worsen, and finally we lost his pulse. He was no more. I was shocked, in immense pain, and felt very depressed. I called my father and said, "Father, today while performing a surgery I lost a patient. I am a doctor and am supposed to save people from dying and not end up killing them. If I cannot save them then I don't deserve to be in this profession". My father was quiet for some time and then replied, "You did your best, Rohan. You are a surgeon and not God. Your job is to help people. God is responsible for one's birth and death. Whatever you do is as per God's wish. This was God's wish and no power can challenge this. So don't be sad, you are just an ordinary human being doing your duty and the ultimate decision God takes from above the clouds". I heard him and disconnected the call. I felt better but still had that guilt.

My dear friend, Surbhi, I would say she is a lot to me than a friend, a heart surgeon. She was fair skinned, tall and slightly chubby with dimple on her right cheek whenever she smiled. She had big eyes which used to speak more than her mouth. By nature, she was very talkative and outspoken. We had been good friends for the past 6 months. To announce my feelings to her, one day I asked her if she could join me for dinner. After thinking for a while, she agreed. We decided to meet at a restaurant which was in the city mall. I was going to propose to her. Thinking how to make this evening more special, I thought of arranging a champagne bottle and a violin player to make the feeling more intense. I briefed the restaurant manager about the arrangements and he gave me the assurance that he will do his best to make my evening beautiful.

Wearing a black suit and a tie, I was waiting for her at the restaurant gate. I saw her walking towards me, and my heartbeat increased. I could feel the air passing through my ears. She looked at me and asked, "Is it a business meeting or are we going to attend a wedding?" All I was doing was blushing! I was behaving very weird. The only thing I was doing was smiling, but why? I don't know either. I was smiling when I was opening the door of the restaurant. Upon reaching the table which I had booked, I pulled the chair so she could sit comfortably. She was impressed and smiled as a gesture. I was so nervous that I started adjusting my underwear. I behaved just like a moron, I didn't know what the hell I was doing and why? Offering her to eat bread, I held a water bottle and when offering her water, I found myself holding bread. Things were going head over heels! She looked at me and asked, "Are you feeling okay? Why are you wearing this suit in the month of May? Can't you see you are sweating! What is wrong with you? Are you under the influence of drugs or something?" I looked at the left and then towards the right and said, "Yes. I am under the influence of drugs and the drug's name is Surbhi". Her eyes were wide open. "I am drugged by your eyes, lips, and your smile. Since the day I met you I am suffering from insomnia, all I do in bed is dream of you with my eyes wide open. Oh Surbhi, I want you in my life, I… I love you Surbhi!" I took out the diamond ring I had bought for her, went on my knees, and said, "I want to see you every morning and night, I want to spend the rest of my life with you, I want you to be the mother of my kids. Surbhi, will you marry me?" Surbhi froze for a moment, she couldn't believe it. She had tears in her eyes. She jumped and kissed me and said, "Yes! Of course, I will marry you!" The whole restaurant was cheering and clapping, and when she looked around all the other guests were standing. I was speechless, in tears and was murmuring. Surbhi was quietly watching and smiling. We had dinner together, and I offered her ride to her hostel. I was still shivering, and I was unable to talk. I could see Surbhi was quiet and looking outside the window, but she had a smile on her face.

Months have passed and we used to see each other every day. We used to have lunch together at the hospital canteen, go on shopping, movies and other recreation activities sometimes with friends but mostly together. I was at home and the doorbell rang. It is Surbhi. Meeting her in the evening, it was a surprise for me as I never expected her to come to my home at this hour. She used to come over but always for a short time mostly during the daytime. Sitting at home we discussed almost everything and now we were out of the conversation. There were a few times that we were sitting and discussing nothing. It was late in the night and I didn't prepare anything for dinner. I called the restaurant and ordered the food Surbhi liked. After finishing the meal, I asked her to get ready so I could drop her at the hostel. "It is too late now, the gates are closed, and they will not allow me to enter in the hostel. Can I stay at your place? If you have a problem I can go to a hotel for a night". I could feel butterflies in my stomach. Extremely naughty thoughts were coming into my head and I was trying to shun them. But I needed to be ready, so I went to the medical shop to buy some last-minute protectors. I was literally running and within 15 minutes I was at home. I offered her my T-Shirt and a pajama from my closet. She went to the other room to change her clothes. I could feel strange things in me. The thoughts were predominating my head and I was slapping my face trying to evade those ideas and thoughts. But when she entered the room I had to rush to the bathroom! Coming back from the bathroom a bit exhausted due to my performance there, she was sitting on the bed watching TV. I couldn't resist and had to retire back to the bathroom. After re-performing my activity, I sat on the bed and started watching the same channel she was watching. I could feel a hand touching my hand. Frightened I looked at her as she removed her clothes. I never have seen such a beautiful girl in my life. all her assets were in the right shape and she started kissing me. In no time I also started kissing, and there was no turning back. After sometime we were lying on the bed breathing heavily but again, we started loving each other the whole night. In the morning I took her to the hostel, there she changed her clothes and we drove to the hospital. Every evening she used to come to my house and from the house in the morning we drove to the hospital. I asked her to leave the hostel and live with me. "My parents won't allow. They don't even know that I am in a relationship with you and I am sleeping here. If they will come to know they would kill me". I looked at her and said, "My parents are cool, but I also don't know how they will react if they come to know about this live-in-relationship!"

After a year, Surbhi suddenly started avoiding me. I thought it might be because of work stress. But when I asked her the reason for this, she would avoid it. She didn't meet me for over a month now. At the hospital also, she pretends to be busy and refuses to meet me. I knew something was wrong but didn't know what it was, this made me very furious. As a result, I too started talking very rudely with people around me including my parents. One day I received a text message from her, "I have resigned from this hospital and I am shifting back. Do not call or text me from today onwards. If you try doing so, I will make an official police complaint against you". I was baffled so I decided to call her. "I think you have not understood what I wrote to you Rohan! I made a mistake loving you and now I am correcting myself," she said. While crying I asked, "But what wrong have I done to you? I love you and I don't want to lose you Surbhi" I started crying more loudly. She disconnected the phone and when I tried to redial her number, she had switched it off. I started punching the wall till I was bleeding, and feeling very helpless. I was dying inside every day thinking about her, crying out loud till my tears went dry. I was cursing myself for the mistake which I didn't even know I had committed. Sometimes I could feel that my reason for living has been snatched and I wanted to commit suicide. I couldn't eat, sleep, or even work. I even stopped answering the calls from my parents, and they started calling me every hour. On Sunday, my parents gave me a surprise visit. I was missing her, so much that my beard had grown big, my hair was all over my face, my eyes were swollen and had grown very thin. Looking at me in this position, my father asked, "What the hell is wrong with you Rohan?" "Did you lose your job, beta?" My mother asked. I was quiet. "Are you heartbroken?" my father asked and there I started crying. They looked at each other and my mother hugged me. "All will be good my son, that girl will regret that she lost you. You are one of a kind," she was trying to console me, but I was still crying. My mother prepared food for the afternoon and in the evening my father brought chilled beer and glasses. "Come sit here Rohan. Let's be friends today." I looked at him. He never spoke to me like this. We were always like father and son. I looked at him and asked "Father, am I not a good man? She said that she made a mistake loving me! If I am a very bad person, why should I be alive? Remember, I killed one of my patients? I don't have the right to live", and I started crying again. My father tapped my head and said "Firstly, stop crying like a baby! You are a man and real men don't cry. Now, listen to me very clearly, you never killed anyone. We discussed this and we both agreed that it was not you, but it was the action of God that killed him. Secondly, this is her mistake that she left you! One day she will be very sorry. Mark my words son, she will. I am sure today or tomorrow she will regret and may try to return to your life. You are not bad at all". I looked at him and hugged him. We had our beer, ate our food and they both went to their room. I was sitting in the balcony and was thinking about her and about this conversation, I loved my parents, knowing that I am not their real child, they came all the way from their home to see me, they always made sure to see that I am protected.

Time passed by but my love for Surbhi didn't change a bit. Every day she wakes me up in my dreams. The hope of seeing her is still deep, still staying with me. Father had to go back due to some work commitment, while mother was looking after me like a small child. From morning tea, breakfast, lunch box, to dinner she was preparing everything herself. Even though I had hired a full-time maid, she always opted to prepare food herself for me. We had a maid for everyday cleaning, but my mother was not happy with her. She always complained about her work and wanted me to remove her. My parents are my strength. When my father returned, I requested to take them to a restaurant for dinner. They kept saying it's a waste of money, but I was strong on it, and finally, they agreed. At the restaurant, we were having our dinner when I suddenly saw Surbhi. She was staring at me and when I turned my head towards her, I could see her leaving the restaurant. I chased her, but she was gone. I shared this with my parents, but they asked me to relax. "It might be someone else. Just because you are thinking about her a lot, it might be that you are mistaken." my mother said. "I am sure it was Surbhi, I can never mistake her for anyone," I thought to myself. That night I couldn't stop thinking about her. Her face at the restaurant was showing up every time I tried closing my eyes. I was missing her a lot. The feelings that I tried to bury inside me were suddenly out. I was feeling depressed, and I cried the whole night and had a headache the following day. At the hospital parking, while reversing my car to the designated parking slot, I saw her again. I jumped out of my car and started brisk walking towards her as she was walking quickly towards the opposite direction. I started running towards her, but she was gone, disappeared into thin air. "There is something wrong somewhere", I said to myself while going back to the hospital. Checking with her colleagues and friends I learned that she never contacted any of them and no one even knew if she was back in town. I was getting suspicious and started to be on alert.

A few days later, I received a call from an unknown number. When I answered the call there was a silence for a second and then the call got disconnected. Immediately I called back on that number. That call was from a PCO, but when I asked who had called me and where that PCO was . I jumped off my bed and ran towards the door. It was the same PCO shop which is in my society. He said that there was a lady who had come and might have called.  I ran down the stairs as fast as I could. I didn't want to miss her now. I asked the PCO person the direction in which she went, and raced towards that direction. While running, I was crying. I was dying to meet her, touch her, and hear her voice. Feeling miserable I reached home and sat in one place. The next morning while driving to the hospital, I was thinking about the good times we had together, all those beautiful memories were going through my eyes and then I received another call, it was again from an unknown number. On answering the call, tears were dripping from my eyes, on the other side of the phone was Surbhi. She asked me to meet her right then. I turned my car towards the location she asked me to.

Reaching there I could see her. As beautiful as she was before she left me. I was feeling very happy and emotional but then the breakup words were in my head and I was having a mixed feeling of joy and bitterness. "What made you come back to my life? Why did you do this to me? What wrong have I done to you? You said you made a mistake loving me" I asked. "You did nothing Rohan, I had to leave you", Surbhi replied. "My parents came to know about my frequent overnight staying at your place. My warden complained to them about it. My parents do not want me to marry you and asked me to marry someone else they had decided. We used to have constant fights and one day my father threatened to disown me. I love my parents very much and couldn't accept this. So, I had to leave you. Knowing that you will not understand my position, I started ignoring you and when I felt that this was not helping, I sent you that message and insulted you over the phone", Surbhi continued. "But deep down, I was crying. I cried every day for you Rohan, I love you a lot", she said while crying.

Seven months ago, I met that boy with whom my father had already fixed my marriage. Everything went well and then I agreed for this marriage not because I loved him but just to keep my parents happy. A month ago, while returning from shopping I got raped. God was kind that they spared my life, but this society rejected me. That boy who was supposed to marry me broke the marriage and my father is still blaming this on me. Nowhere to go, and the only hope for me was you. I wanted to meet you, but I saw you with your parents and I backed out. Many times, I tried to meet you, but I didn't have the courage to face you". Just looking at her I was feeling sorry for her, but I was short of words. "Should I slap her or just hug her, what should I do?" I was thinking. "Whatever happened to you is not correct and I am sorry for you," I replied. Surbhi said while leaving the place, "Just felt like sharing with you, so I did. There is no expectation".

I didn't stop her. I wanted to take my time to think about this and take the consent from my parents. I went home and my mother was waiting for me. I shared with her my meeting and discussion with Surbhi. "Do you love her?" she asked. "Yes, I love her more than anything else in this world. I think I won't be able to survive without her and I was thinking the same till now, but now when I have met her again, I am feeling good" I said. "Then what is the problem? You love her and she loves you, simple?" my mother asked in confusion. "She was raped" I replied. My mother looked at me and said, "Are you blaming her for this? Is it something that she wanted to happen to her, in fact to anyone? What happened to her is a crime and if you are behaving so harsh with her, I feel pity for you". I looked at her and said, "It is easier said than done mother". "Rohan, you were begging on the streets, but we accepted you. You are not our child but still, we loved you like our own. Never judge anyone especially when you know it is not his or her fault. You need to grow with your thoughts and not just with your age". I was convinced and agreed to her. I called my father and told him the same thing. He also reacted the same way my mother did. I was thinking about Surbhi's well-being, her mental stress and the trauma she must have been through. My love for her increased more. Talking over the phone, we decided to meet again at the same restaurant where I had proposed her. The first thing I did was hug her hard and assure her that I was with her. She began to cry, and she said that she knew that I am the person who would understand her and love her the most. I even appreciated my parents who supported me for all this. The same evening, I invited her to my place for dinner. Mother met her and she really loved her. When Surbhi was leaving she even gifted her a pair of gold bangles.

Surbhi wanted to get married without her family getting involved but I and my parents refused. We wanted to have even her family's approval for this marriage, and they decided to go there personally and get the approval for this marriage. Everything was prepared and a day was decided for the meeting between our families. I bought a new saree for my mother and a shirt for my father. I wanted them to look the best. Surbhi's hometown was very far and the mode of transportation was either a train or flight. They never flew on an airplane, so I purchased flight tickets. For them, it was an unnecessary expense but for me I wanted to flaunt to my patents that I can afford to buy expensive things. On arriving in the hometown, it took another hour to reach her home from the airport. Reaching Surbhi's house, the door was opened by her father. He was a fat short person and bald from the crown. He was wearing a shirt and pants with a sling. He met us in half-hearted manner and seemed not interested in us. On the other hand, her mother was very welcoming. She looked like a confident lady but was shaken by her daughter's incident. During our meeting she was always cursing those people who had committed the crime and was very insecure about Surbhi's future. Her husband, on the other hand, was calm and was less reacting on her cries. After lunch we decided to return to the hotel as we had booked accommodation near the airport. Her mother was very happy with the news of us getting married, but her father was quiet as if he was not bothered.

On the way to the hotel, my father started feeling uneasy. He was complaining about pain in his chest. Reaching the hotel, his condition deteriorated, and we had to rush him to the hospital. The doctor at the hospital pronounced him dead on arrival. The cause of death was a massive heart attack. All of us were shaken by the sudden dismissal of him. My mother couldn't control herself from crying. My real parents died when I wanted them the most and today when I wanted him the most, I lost my him too. His remains were brought back to our hometown and there his last rites were performed. He was my inspiration. Whenever I had a problem, he always had a solution. My mother has become a widow and now she would have to live without him throughout her life. She stopped talking much to me or to anyone around. "Mother, I love you and I care about you. I want you to come with me to my house. We will live together" I said to my mother holding her hand, to which she replied "Beta, this is my house, and this is the place from where my soul will depart. Your father had built this house with his own hands. I can feel him in every corner of this house and I can't leave him alone and go. You carry on with your life. Go back to the hospital, since your patients are waiting for you. I know you love me and will never leave me. Go ahead and don't worry, I will be fine here". I know she will never leave this house and she won't keep herself well here. I hired a full-time maid to look after her before I left her.

Within a few months, my mother also passed away. She couldn't cope up with the loss of her husband. I know they are now together up there and are watching me from there. But here I was, alone again, and devastated! I loved them a lot and missed them like anything.

My parents had a will and as per that, all the properties, funds, etc. were in my name. Way back when my father was alive, he picked a date for the marriage which was 6 months ahead. We got married on that same day, which my father had decided, and my mother gave her blessing to us and we lost her after a month. Those people who loved me like anything gave me more than I had deserved and because of them I was an established doctor. Whatever I have today is only because of them.

 A year later, we were blessed with a baby boy. We gave him my father's name – 'Ashok'. I received an offer from a hospital in the UK and that offer was so lucrative that I couldn't say no. I accepted that offer and now I am migrating there.

The house which belongs to my parents is still there and now a home of many children who deserve the best and not the streets. I and my wife started an NGO to secure the future of those children whose faith was written like mine and I am changing their s the same way as that old man did for me.

# The Mind Set

**73**rd Independence Day, during this Independence speech from the ramparts of Red Fort, Prime Minister Narendra Modi spoke on the need for population control and how population explosion will cause many problems for our future generations. But there is a vigilant section of the public which thinks before bringing a child to the world, whether they can do justice to the child, give them everything she or he wants. They have small families and express their patriotism to the country. Let's learn from them. There is a need for social awareness. We love him and follow him blindly. So why do we fail to follow him on this? For ages I used to read and hear the problems of population explosion, trees are cut down, perishable resources are depleting. The houses where we live have become a cage with one small window facing the wall of another building. The forest have shrunken due to extensive urbanization and wild animals are forced to share their space with us. Our country is the 7th largest country in the world and still, we face space issues, seriously!

Hi, my name is Nikhil and I am a proud citizen of India. I pay my taxes to the government on time, pay my EMI to the banks on time and all the other payments are made on time too. I have never defaulted a single instalment. I live in the NCR (National Capital Region) and trust me the place is a jungle. Not jungle of trees but concrete. Everywhere there are only buildings, roads, and flyovers. We can find small bunches of gardens in the name of green patch. In summers the heat is so much that our shoes melt on the coal tar. During the rainy season due to lack of trees, the water washes away the soil which creates soil erosion, and in winter Smog makes everything difficult to see.

Continuing my introduction, my parents are Hindus and I have three elder sisters. The eldest sister whose nickname at home is 'Badi' is about 10 years older than me. The second one is about 9 years elder and her name is 'Shalini', and the third one who is 5 years elder than meis called 'piyaridi'. I gave her this name because when I was born, she used to look after me just like our mother and I used to call her by this name since I started talking. My father is a businessman, so money was never a problem for us. My grandparents used to live with us, and I remember they used to love me more than my sisters. They used to call me 'Kanhaiya'. My grandmother used to say "Bahut Manato ke baad Bhagvan ne tumhe hamare paas bheja hain. (after long praying to god, we were blessed to have you in our family)". I could see that my sisters, in their childhood, used to dislike me. On every occasion, I used to be showered with more gifts than my sisters. At that time, I used to love it but today I think that was wrong. Everything was prepared by my mother and my sisters used to help her with much enthusiasm but still, I was superior of them. Many years after my grandparents passed away there was an argument between my mother and Badi. During the argument, Badi accused our grandparents for being biased. "They never loved us. They only loved Nikhil! They never wanted us because  they always wanted a boy child. If, we were unwanted why did you give birth to us?" My mother was very furious and asked my sister to go back to her room. My sister in immense anger retired to her room. That was the first time I felt the jealousy in their words. I was sad because at this age I understood that it was not my mistake.

Years have passed and all my sisters are now married. I am living with my parents. One morning, we were having breakfast on the table when my mother said, "I asked the servant how many kids she has, and she replied 6 out of which 2 have died". I thought to myself what kind of a person is she? How easily she gave this statement! My mother continues, "I asked her how many boys she has, and she replied 3, the two who died were girls. God saved my boys, tomorrow they will feed us. Girls will get married and for their marriages, we need to arrange dowry. My sons will get married and they will get the dowry". I asked about her daughter, and she said that "She is yet to get married and therefore she is working hard. Once she gets her daughter married, she can rest". To me this conversation was a very sad situation. "It shows that the whole world wishes only for son and not a girl?" I asked my mother. "If they cannot afford to have kids why do they do it?" To which my father stated, "They are illiterate, the husband works very hard and, in the evening, to get some relaxation they only have one thing to do and the result are kids". My mother added, "This is a male-dominated society where only the male's hard work is noticeable. His wife works in 5 flats, wakes up at 4 am, prepares a meal for her husband, bathes, prepares tea once he wakes up, and rushes to work in our flats. She leaves the society at 7 pm. Her husband's work finishes at 5 pm and from there he goes with his friends to have some drinks. Our maid gets to have tea in our house and eats the leftovers in the afternoon as she doesn't get the time to have her breakfast and prepare lunch". To which my father agreed and said, "That is the difference between them and us. Have you ever seen me going out with my friends and coming home drunk? Or have I ever hit you just like these people do?" I agreed with them. I was blessed to be born in this family that is so educated and respects others. A question is now arising to me. If my parents are so educated and know the repercussions of population explosion, why did they have four children? They could have had only one or just as the advertisement announces, "Hum do hamare do (Two Children Policy)"

This question was spinning in my head and soon I got an opportunity to sit with my mother (I used to go to the office and come very late) for some time. I asked, "Mummy, last week you mentioned that the servant had 6 children and out of which 2 died. You and papa said that they are illiterate, so they had so many children. Why did you and papa have 4 children? I mean you should have had 1 or 2". My mother looked at me and said "If we had 2, then you would not have been sitting here. We wanted to have 2 children, but both were daughters. Your grandmother and grandfather were worried that if we don't have a son their legacy would not be carried further. They asked us to try again and after 3 girls we got you". I was surprised! How is my family different from the maids'? The only difference that I see is that my family can afford 4 children whereas the maid cannot. There is nothing to do with education. The mindset is the real problem. I did not continue the discussion with my mother as I knew it won't get where I was thinking. I started surfing the internet and got the following facts.

The Taj Mahal was built by Shah Jahan. The construction started in 1631 and the Taj Mahal was completed by 1648. This was built in the memory of his wife Mumtaz Mahal. It is said that she died while delivering her 14th child. Well, in those times they had much power but didn't have birth control pills. That was the 17th century and now we are in the 21st century. Things have changed with time, we got independence from the British rule and today we have reached Mars. But one thing hasn't changed, the capacity to reproduce children. We are surrounded by many worries. Once a couple gets married, their countdown for having a child starts. People are scared that their child will be alone in the future and they give birth to one more child and then thinking if they would have disputes in the future and have a bitter relationship, they think of giving birth to another child who will try to mend their feuds. The alternate reason (even told by the maid), if any child dies, there should be someone who would support the family.

Human being is a greedy animal. More hands in the family would bring more money! When a boy gets married, the girl's father needs to fulfill the demands of the boy by gifting money, things, or even properties.

In ancient times dowry was given to the groom and his family in exchange for the bride as a way of ensuring that she is properly taken care of and lives comfortably. This dowry system is one given reason for female infanticide. It is also described as gender-selective killing or 'gendercide'. (While typing this my hands are shivering. It is such a shameful thing to write or even talk about. I wouldn't want to elaborate more on this.)

Researching more on the net I found that the population of India is about 17.7% of the total world's population. The main cities densely populated are Mumbai Delhi Bengaluru and so on. Approximately 67,700 children are born every year in India. China is on the top in population. The total world population is 7,818,176,440 (approx.). I was surprised to read this data but thought how ignorant we were! Despite knowing the problems of the population, we are still going strong.

Once on a Friday evening, my sisters, their husbands, and their kids were at our home for the weekend. My eldest sister "Badi" is married to a doctor. He owns his clinic and visits several renowned hospitals in the city. They have been blessed with 3 children. 2 daughters, and a son. Their son is the youngest. My second sister is married with no children and my third sister has a son and a daughter. Her son was elder than the daughter. This happened to make sure that their son is not alone in this world. As only I, my mother, and my father live here, the house is usually silent. But when kids are here, I can see the house on fire, literally. There is constant shouting in the house, food wrappers are thrown, TV is constantly on, the kitchen is always occupied and most irritating is that one of the kids is always crying! All of us adults, were sitting on the sofa and while having a discussion when my sister Shalini started talking about her friend who was facing a big problem getting admission for her children. She said, "My friend had to make an appointment to meet the principal who would take a simple test of the child before admission. Based on that interaction the school will decide whether the child will get admission. But before this, the school will ask the parents to fill a form in which the basic information of the parents should be filled like their education, profession, and even gross and net income". My sister Badi added, "Each class has at least 30 students with the ratio of 30:1". To this her husband corrected her, " Bihar has the highest student-teacher ratio which is about 50-60:1, followed by Uttar Pradesh, Jharkhand, West Bengal and Madhya Pradesh which are defiantly higher than 30:1 ratio".

When I asked them how they got this detail they asked me to search this on the net and I confirmed if this information and this data may be incorrect.? I understood as I know this information is usually inflated and not very accurate. My sister nodded her head toward me and continued, "The fee is high, uniforms, books, and we have to wake up in the morning to prepare food for them. I never prepared food for my husband (laughing), and he never asked me either. He can see how busy I am, I need to leave by 8 am for work, I cannot do it. I am doing it for my kid that is more than enough. But when my in-laws are there, I have no escape. I have to prepare tea for them and even lunch". To which her husband, in a jolly way, says, "And looking at the tiffin, my colleagues know that my parents have come". All laugh including his wife. After a while, my mother hinted Badi to say something. Looking at my mother, Badi nodded her head and said, "Shalini, these days we have many solutions for those couples who don't have kids, for example, IVF which stands for In- vitro Fertilization. Remember we went to see a movie by Akshay Kumar and Kareena Kapoor in which the film revolves around two couples who want to have their kids through IVF. Don't go on the goof-up of what had happened, that was just for the movie. You should think about it".  Shalini was listening to her very silently. "You don't have to suffer my child", Mother says. "Everything will be fine". Shalini looks at the whole family and says, "Thanks to you all for thinking about me. Firstly, I and my husband are not at all worried about us not able to bring a child of our own. We are enjoying our lives very much and we don't have any added responsibility. Secondly, if in the future we plan to have a child I would adopt a child rather than wasting money on these processes. The money I spend on these, I can spend on some child to make his future". My Mother jumped "Beta, whatever you are saying is very good to hear, but your blood is your blood. A Cuckoo lays its eggs in the crow's nest and the crow takes care of it. When the eggs hatch, it is not a crow but a cuckoo. It will be cuckoo and never be like a crow. It will go ahead and do the same thing its mother did with that crow. So, think before you act". All of the family members agree to both and then my father says, "Let them make their decision. If they want to have their child let them and if they want to adopt let them. You said what you think. Now let them decide". Reacting to this Shalini said, "Don't worry, we know what is better for us and what is not. Thank you for your suggestions but I don't need these".

After hours of discussions, we all retired to our rooms. I was lying on my bed and was thinking if education has become so costly, why the population is still rising? I started net searching on my phone when I found another topic. That was unemployment. According to the website, the rate of unemployment in India is high. Looking at the actual reason why there is unemployment, the top cause was a large population. Here also population is the cause. The country's economic growth cannot keep up with the population growth, which leads to a part of the society being unemployed. The supply of the workforce is much higher than the demand. This is the reason why poverty exists. Searching more on poverty I find that a very high percentage of Indians are unable to have enough food due to unemployment and are even underemployed.  On the websites, I could see infants who were suffering from acute food deficiency. It was scary, I closed that page. I thought to myself, closing the page will not solve the problem. The world should get together and do something serious about the fast-increasing population.

Searching more on the internet, I found a link on global warming. I had heard about it and had a vague idea. When I tapped on the link, I started reading. Here also, the major problem is population. It states, "The rapidly growing population is increasing the pressure on the global environment, threatening its ability to supply itself with an adequate amount of food, water, and fuel and with a quality environment." The burning of fossil fuels and deforestation creates a greenhouse effect in the atmosphere. This gradually increases the temperature which leads to reduced rainfall, etc. which causes global warming. Due to global warming, the ice is melting at a much faster rate which is increasing the sea level. The famous Italian city of Venice is slowly sinking. The average rate of sinking is 1 to 2 mm a year.

If it keeps up with this pace for the next 20 years, it will sink by 80 mm relative to the sea level. The rise in sea level in Mumbai is also visible. These days we can see extreme climate change which is another perfect example of global warming. In Rajasthan, this year, some places were the hottest at 50.8 degrees Celsius, nine notches above normal.

I am forced to think why we are so ignorant about the danger which is coming slowly towards us? Do we know that population is the reason for so many things still we are doing very little or nothing on this? China had introduced the policy of 1 child law. Being so strict on this law still, it is holding its first position in the world and India is still holding the second position, whereas the USA is following up on the third position. Extreme laws are made but, strangely, the result is very disheartening. Who is responsible for this? The government, the people, or the grandparents? I think no one knows because if it was known I am sure this would have been taken care of. With this, I kept my phone aside and slept.

The next day I woke up with the shrieks of a child. Man, it blew my head off! I got dressed and left for the office. Even when it was Saturday, the roads were flooded with cars. I was able to remember the topics I was reading. There was a person on a bike standing next to my car. We were standing at a red light. He was without his helmet. Looking at his face, I could see that he was very disturbed. God knows what his problems are, but I am sure it might be directly or indirectly related to the population. Most of the problems in our lives are due to the population. Someone needs money for his marriage or for paying rent or even to take their loved ones for leisure activity. A bus was so much filled with passengers, if the driver presses sudden breaks, the passengers standing at the gate would fly out like superman. I know it's nothing to make fun of, but also, it's not the right way. The competition is so cut-throat that everyone wants to win over others. See, again because of the population. After 2 hours I reached the office and, in the evening, I left for home. Again, it took me a good two and a half hours reaching home.

Reaching home, I saw my sisters sitting at the dining table. I could sense something was not right. I hurriedly asked them the reason for their concern, and they broke the very sad news. Our family friends, who lived 2 buildings away were found dead in their house. They were an old couple and their kids were living abroad. The news was shocking. They had been murdered. The housemaid in the morning called the cops as she could smell a foul smell coming from the house. The door was closed for about 3 days and she thought that they had gone out to their relative's place. As per the police, it looked like some people broke into the house for burglary and killed the couple. Whether the couple had woken up in the night or the thieves had killed them deliberately, will get confirmed only after their investigation gets over. Discussing with my sisters why they might have done this, Pyaridi said, "The murder had happened only for money and jewelry. The killers broke into the house and demanded money to which the couple might have objected and therefore they might have gotten killed. If they had given everything, they might have been alive". My other sister lightly said, "Yes, it seems that you were with the gang. You know everything how it happened and why", to which my mother in a very afraid voice said, "Shut up. Don't say things like this. If anyone overheard this, they might complain to the police, and the police might arrest her". We all burst with laughter and I said, "Mother, you are such a naive person. Nothing of that sort will happen. And even if something of that sort happens you can go every day to the police station to deliver her food". Pyaridi jumped with excitement and said, "Yes mother, please do so, the food in jail is so bad I will not be able to eat". My mother was angry and staring at us.

What had happened to our family friends was not a good thing and was nothing to joke about. But you know, house humour has nothing to do with real issues! Thinking about why they would enter an unknown house, steal things, and kill somebody, reflects the dark side of unemployment, and unemployment is due to population. The backbone of all the issues is population. The cause of crime is complex. Poverty, parental neglect, alcohol, and drug abuse are the main reasons for crimes. All these reasons are directly or indirectly related to population. We are not only responsible for ourselves or to our families but also responsible for nature. If we are the ones who have destroyed it then it should be our responsibility to mend it again.

Soon, the police were able to catch hold of the killers. The police was interrogating them for 3 days and then the court case that was filed against them had also started. It was later revealed that they were father and son. The father was a thief for ages, but his son was working in a company. His expenses couldn't be met with the salary he used to get so he joined his father to earn more. Our maid knew them. She was the one who told us all this. My mother asked her more about them to which she said, "The son has two wives and 6 children and his parents were living together with them. He married his first wife and had 2 children and then he fell in love with her sister and he got married to her too. From her, he has 4 children. He is a very hardworking person but with such a big family he needed to get more money. He doesn't want both his wives to work, so they are at home. His father is a thief and now and then he is found in jail. His son was forced to do this crime.

Now, I am 25 years old. I have a girlfriend and we are going to get married soon. I am working in a good company with a good package and Hina (my girlfriend) is also working in a company with a good package. We both purchased a house together and will shift once we get married. The house is on loan and both of us are splitting the EMI. We decided in the beginning that both of us will be responsible for all the work in and around the house. If Hina prepares the food, I will wash the utensils and if I buy the groceries, Hina will do the laundry. Even the bigger expenses like EMIs of the house, cars, or other things and our salaries will be equally divided. Neither I nor she believes in the old tales where the females are responsible for the house chores while males will bring home money. Both of us will work together on both the fronts- house and professional. This is nothing special we are doing. All our friends are doing the same thing. I think our generation has the decency to respect the females and give them the same respect and position as we males get. The important point is children. I and Hina decided to have only one child. It won't matter if it's a boy or a girl. We are going to accept it. The next important point is the dowry. My mother's thinking is like my grandmother's, she thinks the tradition should continue from generation to generation and me not accepting is breaking it. As per her, we gave at the time of my sister's then why not now? She asked for a small thing just for the sake of the tradition, but I was very firm that this tradition shouldn't be there at all. My father intervened between me and my mother. He said, "When the children have decided that dowry will not happen then it will not. Why are you forcing them, this generation is more modern! In the western world there is nothing like dowry, so it won't happen. Like they are doing with Holi and Deepawali. Suddenly after years, they are thinking about nature. One day we celebrate with crackers the world is polluted. Every day when they fire the engines of cars, pollution emissions are nothing compared to the festival. Right, Nikhil? You have grown big and now you will decide everything. Why don't you just marry the girl and come home? Nowadays your generation is doing court marriages! Why waste money and that huge amount?" "Traditions go with generations and not with your mood. You are Hindu and Hindu's have their own traditions. We are not westerners, lighting candles and singing Christmas carols or hymns. For god sake, do not let our tradition die". Saying this father leaves for his room. What my father said is partially correct and partially wrong. Indian festivals are awesome. We all enjoyed it when we were kids. At that time the whole country used to enjoy and celebrate but these days it has reduced to a limited section in the society. But comparing dowry with our festivals is not correct. Dowry is a blackspot on our face. It is responsible for millions of female foeticides. Now, if things are changing it's done for good. We need to eliminate this from our lives and our traditions. When the government has categorized dowry as a criminal offense why we cannot accept it and avoid it?

Days before my marriage, the whole family decided to go shopping. We had an amazing time. I, my sisters and my parents were all together shopping after ages. I don't even remember when we all went the last time. The shops were having huge discounts due to marriage season and all of us were shopping endlessly. While roaming across the street I could see beggars begging for money. Some of them were blind, some were handicapped. I could find many of all ages. I can see other people working as potters, rickshaw pullers moving around. All of them are not happy. They are living a very difficult life. What they will eat tonight will be decided with the money they earn. If they don't earn well enough, they will have an onion and bread and if they earn well, they may have non-veg. The food which we eat every day and never appreciate is a delicacy for them. They know the real meaning of money and how to appreciate whatever they get to eat. We eat pizza or burger to change our taste whereas they eat pizza or burgers to celebrate a very big thing and they can only afford if they have got a good amount of money. They are also suffering because of the population explosion. We completed our shopping and, on our way, back to our cars, I was stopped by a beggar. A young girl, I guess a 10- or 11-year old child, came to me and begged for some money. I refused and started ahead when I heard her saying "Please help me by giving money. I am very hungry. I will die of starvation". I felt bad and returned to her. I took her to a small restaurant and asked the owner of that restaurant to feed her. I gave him some money and he asked his helper to bring her food I could see her eating. She did not look upwards but only eat the food. I was feeling very happy and proud of feeding a small girl who is not at all responsible for the situation.

The day has come and today is my marriage. I am sitting on a horse and my family is dancing ahead of me. I can see the happiness in their eyes. My friends and colleagues are also among the people who are dancing in the middle and then disappear. They go to the car standing behind which is full of whiskey and cigarettes. So, after dancing they will go back to wet their throats and get some fuel to enjoy. The marriage has gone well, and we have completed all the ceremonies. While boarding the car to return with my wife, I saw her father giving a bag to my father. My father refused and said, "You have given me your daughter and that is what I only want". I felt so proud of my parents. He did not accept it. Reaching home, we played some games and then we left for a hotel which was booked for our first night.

The deal is now on. Whatever we decided before our marriage is now working correctly. All the bills are paid as we had decided. Few things went out of control initially but now after one year of our marriage, those issues have subsided. The new point now was a child. We are now trying for a child. Thinking about the population, where there are millions of babies born every day, I think my baby also deserves to come to this world correct? Yes, so Hina is now pregnant. At home, Hina and I don't have any topic other than discussing about our child. We go for shopping and keep buying things which may be useful when Hina is at the hospital and once our baby is born. Hina wants a boy and I want a daughter. In India, the determination of sex of a child is illegal, so it will be a boy or a girl is a mystery till then. Once a month she must visit the doctor and I always go along with her. At the hospital, while waiting for our turn to meet the doctor I can see only new expecting parents. This is only one of the hospitals in the city and out of 6 hours of consultation this is only the first hour, and there are so many pregnant women. Now, I can see a huge number which is seriously concerning. But I deserve to have one child! The consulting days go well, and the day has come for my baby to arrive in this world. And here she comes. I am very happy. I have become a father. We have been blessed with a daughter. I and Hina name her Parulwhich means, a five-petaled flower known for its beauty. It is also a unisex name of Hindu origin.

Parul is now 2 years old and my parents are concerned that we don't have a son. The day Parul will get married her surname will be changed and our family tree will come to an end! Every other day I would receive a call from my parents and in every discussion, the boy baby is always included. It was getting on us both. While discussing Hina said, "Parul is our only child. All around us there are siblings. Parul will feel lonely as she won't have a brother. I think we should have 2 babies one daughter and one son". I thought over this and there was no harm in that. As we decided we started the process for our second baby. The whole long process of 9 months was repeated. Hina was back at the hospital and the nurse rushed out and announced that we have been blessed with another baby girl. I was happy. Very happy but only one thing rushed in my mind that we wanted a boy and we got a girl again. My parents were happy but not as much as they would if it was a son. We decided to call her Priyanka. Priyanka is derived from the Sanskrit word 'Priyankera' or 'Priyankara', meaning someone or something amiable, lovable, or makes you happy and very talkative.

Years passed and my parents are still not happy. They wanted a boy. They are sad that this family will end with me. I and Hina are happy with our children. Now, Hina and I have started to discuss again having one more child. We both decided to have another. This time it may be a boy. The whole process restarted, and the day has come after 9 months. The stress is for our third child. "This should be our last child. But what happens if we get another daughter?" I was scared as these thoughts were going within me. I didn't know what to do! Finally, I come to know that this time it was a boy. I was relieved. At last, we got a boy. All my family, relatives, and friends were called to give this news. My parents called him "Arjun" which is an Indian male name, based on Arjuna, a legendary hero who is the best archer and the central character of the Hindu epic Mahabharata. Now my parents were happy, because they can see that their family tree branching ahead. Somewhere even I and Hina wanted a son. Now, the family is complete and now we can focus on their education.

Even though we know that our actions are directly or indirectly affecting nature, we commit those actions. We all are responsible for all the things which are negatively affecting the earth. Be it natural resources depleting, deforestation, soil erosion, earthquakes, tsunami, floods, etc, are all because of us. We are multiplying at such a great pace that animals are now thrown out of their habitat so we can build ours. Every day there are animals killed not for food but only because they entered human society. They did not, we did. We are responsible for these animals to come out and attack us. We are responsible for imbalance in the ecosystem. We all need to think about it as today's encounters with animals will be tomorrow's exciting fairy tales for the next generations. We still have time, but we don't have much space. Together let's think and act on how to reduce today to save tomorrow not for us but for the next generation.